25.50

THE JOY LUCK CLUB

... between a mother and ... It goes ... others can reach and continues beyond the grave. During life, however, it may not be at all comfortable; there may be battles and misunderstandings, impatience and anger. And if your mother was born in pre-Revolutionary China, and you were born in San Francisco in the 1950s, a child of two widely differing cultures, how do you explain your problems to her? How will she understand your feelings?

Jing-mei, Waverly, Lena, and Rose grow up speaking English and drinking Coca-Cola, free to choose their jobs, their life-styles, and their husbands. But they also carry the hopes and expectations of their mothers, who left unspeakable sorrows behind them in China to travel to America, a country where their children will have choices that were denied to them. But it is also a country of change and confusion, a place where the Chinese idea of 'joy luck' does not mean the same to an American-born mind.

Each mother and daughter tells her own story, except for Jing-mei's mother, who has just died. Now Jing-mei nervously takes her mother's place at the Joy Luck Club, sitting at the mah jong table on the East corner, the direction from which the sun rises, where the wind comes from, where things begin . . .

OXFORD BOOKWORMS LIBRARY

Human Interest

The Joy Luck Club

Stage 6 (2500 headwords)

Series Editor: Jennifer Bassett
Founder Editor: Tricia Hedge
Activities Editors: Jennifer Bassett and Christine Lindop

To my mother
and the memory of her mother

You asked me once
what I would remember.

This, and much more.

AMY TAN

The Joy Luck Club

Retold by
Clare West

OXFORD UNIVERSITY PRESS

OXFORD

UNIVERSITY PRESS

Great Clarendon Street, Oxford OX2 6DP

Oxford University Press is a department of the University of Oxford.
It furthers the University's objective of excellence in research, scholarship,
and education by publishing worldwide in

Oxford New York

Auckland Cape Town Dar es Salaam Hong Kong Karachi
Kuala Lumpur Madrid Melbourne Mexico City Nairobi
New Delhi Shanghai Taipei Toronto

With offices in

Argentina Austria Brazil Chile Czech Republic France Greece
Guatemala Hungary Italy Japan Poland Portugal Singapore
South Korea Switzerland Thailand Turkey Ukraine Vietnam

OXFORD and OXFORD ENGLISH are registered trade marks of
Oxford University Press in the UK and in certain other countries

Original edition © Amy Tan 1989
First published in Great Britain by William Heinemann Ltd 1989
This simplified edition © Oxford University Press 2008

Database right Oxford University Press (maker)

First published in Oxford Bookworms 2002

2 4 6 8 10 9 7 5 3

ISBN 978 0 19 479263 9

Printed in Hong Kong

ACKNOWLEDGEMENTS
Illustrated by: David Frankland
Chinese calligraphy by: James Lin

This edition is reprinted by arrangement with G.P. Putnam's Sons,
a member of Penguin Group (USA) Inc.

Word count (main text): 31,120 words

For more information on the Oxford Bookworms Library,
visit www.oup.com/elt/bookworms

CONTENTS

PEOPLE IN THIS STORY

THE MOTHERS

Suyuan Woo

An-mei Hsu

Lindo Jong

Ying-ying St Clair

THE DAUGHTERS

Jing-mei 'June' Woo

Rose Hsu Jordan

Waverly Jong

Lena St Clair

NOTE ON THE LANGUAGE

The mothers in this story speak a variety of English that uses non-standard forms (for example, omitting articles or auxiliary verbs). This feature has been retained in the adaptation as it is a powerful reminder of the cultural transitions in the story, both between countries and also between first- and second-generation Americans.

Feathers from a Thousand Miles Away

THE OLD WOMAN *remembered a swan she had paid too much for, many years ago in Shanghai. This bird, boasted the market seller, was once a duck that stretched its neck in hopes of becoming something better, and now look! – it is too beautiful to eat.*

Then the woman and the swan sailed across an ocean many thousands of miles wide, stretching their necks towards America. On her journey she whispered to the swan: 'In America I will have a daughter just like me. But over there nobody will say her worth is measured by the loudness of her husband's belch. Over there nobody will look down on her, and she will always be too full to swallow any sorrow! She will know my meaning, because I will give her this swan.'

But when she arrived in the new country, the officials pulled her swan away from her, leaving the woman with only one swan feather for a memory. And then she had to answer so many questions that she forgot why she had come and what she had left behind.

Now the woman was old. And she had a daughter who grew up speaking only English and swallowing more Coca-Cola than sorrow. For a long time now the woman had wanted to give her daughter the single swan feather and tell her, 'This feather may look worthless, but it comes from a long way away and carries with it all my good intentions.'

And she waited, year after year, for the day she could tell her daughter this in perfect American English.

The Joy Luck Club

My father has asked me to be the fourth player at the Joy Luck Club. I am replacing my mother, whose seat at the mah jong table has been empty since she died two months ago. My father thinks she was killed by her own thoughts.

'She had a new idea inside her head,' said my father. 'But the thought grew too big and burst. It must have been a very bad idea.'

The doctor said she died because a blood vessel in the brain swelled up and burst. And her friends at the Joy Luck Club said she died just like a rabbit under the wheels of a car: quickly and with unfinished business left behind. My mother was supposed to host the next meeting of the Joy Luck Club.

She had started the San Francisco Joy Luck Club in 1949, two years before I was born. This was the year my parents left China with one large leather case filled only with fine silk dresses. There was no time to pack anything else, my mother had explained to my father after they boarded the boat. Still his hands swam desperately between the slippery silks, looking for his cotton shirts.

When they arrived in San Francisco, my father made her hide those shiny clothes. She wore the same brown Chinese dress every day, until she was given two second-hand dresses by the white-haired ladies from the local church. Because of these and other gifts, my parents could not refuse the old ladies' invitation to join the church. Nor could they ignore the ladies' practical advice to improve their English by attending religious study classes on Wednesday nights. This was how my parents met the Hsus, the Jongs, and the St Clairs. My mother could sense that the women of these families also had unspeakable sorrows they had left behind in China, and hopes they couldn't begin to express in their broken English. Or at least she recognized the deadness in these women's faces. And she saw how quickly their eyes moved when she told them her idea for the Joy Luck Club.

Joy Luck was an idea my mother remembered from the days of her first marriage in a town called Kweilin, before the Japanese invasion. That's why I think of Joy Luck as her Kweilin story. It was the story she would always tell me when she was bored, when every bowl had been washed and the plastic-covered table had been wiped down twice, when my father sat reading the newspaper and smoking one cigarette after another, a warning not to disturb him. Then my mother would start her story. Over the years, she told me the same story, except for the ending, which grew darker, throwing long shadows into her life, and eventually into mine.

'I dreamed about Kweilin before I ever saw it,' my mother began, speaking Chinese. 'I dreamed of high mountains, surrounded by white mists. If you reached the top, you would be able to see everything and feel such happiness that you would never have worries in your life ever again.

'In China, everybody dreamed about Kweilin. And when I arrived, I realized how thin my dreams were, how poor my thoughts. When I saw the hills, I laughed and trembled at the same time. They were so strange and beautiful that you can't even imagine them.

'But I didn't come to Kweilin to see how beautiful it was. The man who was my husband brought me and our two babies there, because he thought we would be safe. He was an officer in the army, and after he had found a small room for us, he left us and went off to fight in Chungking, in the northwest.

'We all knew the Japanese were winning, even when the newspapers said they were not. Every day, every hour, thousands of people poured into Kweilin, trying to escape from the fighting. Rich and poor, Chinese and foreign, religious and political, we were all kinds of people mixed together. Everybody looked down on someone else. It didn't matter that we all lived in the same dirt and had the same illnesses. We all smelt just as bad as each other, but everybody complained that someone else smelt the worst.

'So you can see how quickly Kweilin lost its beauty for me. I no longer said, How lovely these hills are! I only wondered which hills the Japanese had reached. I sat in the dark corners of my house with a baby under each arm, waiting with nervous feet. And when we were warned of the approach of the bombers, my neighbours and I hurried to the deep caves to hide like wild animals. But you can't stay in the dark for long. You become like a starving person, crazy-hungry for light. Can you imagine how it is, to want to be neither inside nor outside, to want to be nowhere and disappear?

'I thought of Joy Luck one unbearably hot summer night. Every place was so crowded and smelly that there was no room for fresh air. At all hours of the day and night I heard screams. I didn't know if they came from animals or humans. I didn't go to the window to find out. What use would that have been? And that's when I decided I needed something to do.

'My idea was to have a gathering of four women, one for each corner of my mah jong table. I had a beautiful mah jong table, from my family, made of very fine wood. Each week one of us women would host a party to make us all feel more cheerful. The hostess had to serve special foods to bring good luck of all kinds – money, good health, the birth of sons, and long life.

'What fine food we allowed ourselves, on so little money! We pretended not to notice that the vegetables were stringy and the fruit was half-eaten by insects. We knew we were luckier than most people. After filling our stomachs, we would fill a bowl with money, and then we would sit down at the mah jong table. Once we started to play, nobody could speak. We had to concentrate on our game, and think of nothing else but adding to our happiness through winning. But after our game, we would eat again, this time to celebrate our good fortune. And then we would talk into the night until the morning, telling stories – oh, what wonderful stories! – about good times in the past and good times yet to come.

'People thought we were wrong to serve up these meals every week, when many in Kweilin were starving. Others thought we were wicked, to celebrate when even within our own families we had lost relations, homes and fortunes. Hnnh! How could we laugh? people asked.

'It's not that we had no heart or eyes for pain. We were all afraid. We all had our miseries. But what was worse, we asked ourselves, to sit and wait for our own deaths with proper serious faces? Or to choose our own happiness?

'So we decided to hold parties and pretend each week had become the new year. Each week we could forget past sufferings. We weren't allowed to think a bad thought. We ate, we laughed, we played games, lost and won, we told the best stories. And each week, we could hope to be lucky. That hope was our only joy. And that's how we came to call our little parties Joy Luck.'

My mother always ended the story on a happy note, boasting about her skill at the game. 'I won many times and was so lucky that the others said I had learnt a clever thief's tricks! I won so much money! But of course I wasn't rich, because by then paper money had become worthless.'

I never thought my mother's Kweilin story was true, because the endings always changed. Sometimes she said she used her worthless winnings to buy a half-cup of rice; other times it was pig's feet, or eggs, or chickens. The story grew and grew. And then one evening, when I was a teenager, she told me a completely different end to the story.

'An army officer came to my house early one morning and told me to leave Kweilin as soon as possible. I knew the Japanese must be close. But how could I leave? There were no trains. My neighbour was so good to me. She bribed a man to steal a wheelbarrow, and promised to warn my other friends.

'I packed my things and my two babies into this wheelbarrow, and began pushing it towards Chungking. On the fourth day I heard, from people running past me on the road, that the Japanese had marched into Kweilin and killed hundreds of the inhabitants. When I heard this news, I walked faster and faster.

'I went on pushing until my wheel broke. I abandoned my beautiful mah jong table. By then I didn't have enough feeling in my body to cry. I carried a baby tied to each shoulder and a bag in each hand, one with clothes, the other with food. I finally dropped one bag after the other when my hands began to bleed and became too slippery to hold onto anything.

'As I went on, I saw that others had done the same, gradually given up hope. The road was covered with beautiful things that grew in value along the way. By the time I arrived in Chungking I had lost everything except for three fine silk dresses, which I wore one on top of the other.'

'What do you mean by "everything"?' I gasped at the end. I

I didn't have enough feeling in my body to cry.

was shocked to realize the story had been true all the time. 'What happened to the babies?'

She didn't even pause to think. She simply said in a way that made it clear there was no more to the story: 'Your father is not my first husband. You are not those babies.'

When I arrive at the Hsus' house, where the Joy Luck Club is meeting tonight, the first person I see is my father. 'There she is! Never on time!' he announces. And it's true. Everybody's already here, seven family friends in their sixties and seventies. They look up and laugh at me, always late, a child still at thirty-six.

I'm shaking, trying to hold in my feelings. The last time I saw them, at the funeral, I broke down and cried. They must wonder how someone like me can take my mother's place. A friend once told me that my mother and I were alike. When I shyly told my mother this, she seemed insulted and said, 'You don't even know little percent of me! How can you be me?' And she's right. How can I be my mother at Joy Luck?

'Auntie, Uncle,' I say, nodding to each person there. I have always called these old family friends Auntie and Uncle.

Tonight we are all seated round the dining room table, as Uncle George puts on his glasses and starts reading the minutes:

'In our account we have $24,825. We sold Subaru for a loss at $6000. We bought a hundred shares of Smith International at $7000. Our thanks to Lindo and Tin Jong for the meal. The soup was especially delicious. The March meeting had to be canceled. We were sorry to have to say a fond goodbye to our dear friend Suyuan. Our sympathy to the Woo family.'

That's all. I keep thinking the others will start talking about my mother and the wonderful friendship they shared. But they all just nod to approve the minutes. And it seems to me my mother's life has been forgotten, to make way for new business.

Auntie An-mei gets up slowly and walks heavily to the kitchen to prepare the food, while the others discuss financial matters. I follow her to ask why they started buying shares.

'We used to play mah jong, winner take all,' she says. 'But the same people were always winning, the same people always losing. You can't have luck when someone else has skill. So, long time ago, we decided to buy and sell shares. No skill in that. Even your mother agreed. Now we can all win and lose equally. And we can play mah jong for fun, winner take all. Loser take home uneaten food! Everyone can have some joy. Smart, huh?'

I watch Auntie An-mei making little parcels of meat and vegetables. She has quick, expert fingers, so she doesn't have to think about what she's doing. That's what my mother used to complain about, that Auntie An-mei never thought about what she was doing. I wonder what Auntie An-mei did to make my mother criticize her so much.

But then, my mother seemed to be displeased with all her friends, with me, and even with my father. Something was always missing. Something needed improving. Something was not in balance. There was too much of one element, not enough of another. Each person is made of five elements, she told me.

Too much fire and you had a bad temper. That was like my father, whom my mother criticized for smoking and who always shouted back at her.

Too little wood and you bent too quickly to listen to other people's ideas, unable to stand on your own, like Auntie An-mei.

Too much water and you flowed in too many directions, like me. I started studying science, then changed to art, then worked as a secretary, later becoming a writer for an advertising agency.

'Time to eat,' Auntie An-mei announces happily. There are piles of heavenly-smelling food on the table, and everybody eats as if they are starving. After the meal, the men go to another room to play cards, while the women carry the plates and bowls to the kitchen and put them in the sink. Now we walk through the house to the bedroom at the back, which was once shared by all three Hsu girls. We were childhood friends, but now they've all grown up and married, and I'm here to play in their room again.

Nobody tells me where my mother used to sit. But I can tell, even before everyone sits down. The chair closest to the door has an emptiness to it. But the feeling doesn't really have to do with the chair. Without anyone telling me, I know her corner on the table was the East.

The East is where things begin, my mother once told me, the direction from which the sun rises, and where the wind comes from.

'Do you win like your mother?' asks Auntie Lindo, sitting opposite me. She is not smiling.

'I only played a little in college with American friends.'

'Hnnh! American mah jong,' she says disgustedly. 'Not the same thing.' This is what my mother said when I once asked her the difference between American and Chinese mah jong.

'Completely different kind of playing,' she said in her English explanation voice. 'American mah jong, they watch only for themselves, play only with their eyes.' Then she switched to Chinese: 'Chinese mah jong, you must play using your head, be very clever.'

This kind of explanation made me feel my mother and I spoke two different languages, which we did. I talked to her in English, she talked back in Chinese.

Now we begin to play, in a relaxed, unhurried way. The Joy Luck aunties make conversation, not really listening to each other.

'Oh, I have a story,' says Auntie Ying suddenly. She has always been the strange auntie, someone lost in her own world.

'Police arrested Mrs Emerson's son last weekend,' she says, proud to be the first with the news. 'Too many TV set found in his car. Mrs Chan told me at church.'

Auntie Lindo says quickly, 'Aii-ya, Mrs Emerson good lady,' meaning Mrs Emerson didn't deserve such a terrible son. But now I see this is also for the benefit of Auntie An-mei, whose own son was arrested two years ago for selling stolen stereos.

Auntie Lindo and my mother were best friends and sworn enemies, who spent a lifetime comparing their children. I was one month older than Waverly Jong, Auntie Lindo's prized daughter. From the time we were babies, our mothers compared how fast we grew, how thick and dark our hair was, how many shoes we wore out in a year, and later, how smart Waverly was at playing chess, and how many competitions she had won.

I knew my mother hated listening to Auntie Lindo talk about Waverly when she had nothing to respond with. So at first my mother tried to find my hidden skills. She did housework for a retired piano teacher, who gave me lessons and an old piano to practice on, in exchange. But when I failed to show any musical promise at all, she finally explained that I was a late developer.

'It's getting late,' I say, after the next round, getting up.

'No, no, you must stay!' says Auntie Lindo, pushing me back into the chair. 'We have something important to tell you, from your mother.' The others look uncomfortable, as if this is not how they wanted to break some sort of bad news to me.

I sit down. Auntie An-mei gets up to shut the door. Everybody is quiet, as if nobody knows where to begin.

It is Auntie Ying who finally speaks. 'I think your mother die with important thought on her mind,' she says in broken English. And then in Chinese, calmly and softly, 'Your mother was a very strong woman, a good mother. She loved you very much, more than her own life. You can understand why a mother like this could never forget her other daughters. She knew they were alive, and before she died she wanted to find her daughters in China.'

The babies in Kweilin, I think. I was not those babies. And now my mother's left me forever, gone back to China to get these babies. I can hardly hear Auntie Ying's voice.

'She had searched for years,' says Auntie Ying. 'And last year she got an address. Aii-ya, what a pity. A lifetime of waiting.'

Auntie An-mei interrupts excitedly: 'So your aunties and I, we wrote to this address. And they wrote back to us. They are your sisters, Jing-mei.' My sisters, I repeat to myself, saying these two words together for the first time.

Auntie An-mei is holding out a sheet of writing paper covered in Chinese handwriting. Auntie Ying is handing me another envelope with a check made out to Jing-mei Woo for $1,200. I can't believe it. 'My sisters are sending *me* money?'

'No, no,' says Auntie Lindo. 'Every year we save our mah jong winnings for big dinner at expensive restaurant. We add just a little, so you can go Hong Kong, take train to Shanghai, see your sisters. Besides, we all getting too fat for big dinner.'

'See my sisters,' I repeat stupidly. I know my aunties are lying to mask their generosity. I am crying now, crying and laughing, seeing but not understanding this loyalty to my mother.

'You must tell your sisters about your mother's death,' says Auntie Ying. 'But most important, you must tell them about her life. The mother they did not know, they must now know.'

'But what can I tell them about my mother?' I ask. 'I don't know anything about her. She was my mother.'

'Not know your own mother?' cries Auntie An-mei with disbelief. 'How can you say? She is in your bones!' The aunties all join in, desperate to say what should be passed on.

'Tell them about her kindness, her smartness.'

'Tell them her hopes, things that matter to her.'

'Tell them about the excellent dishes she cooked.'

'Imagine, a daughter not knowing her own mother!'

And then I realize they are frightened. In me, they see their own daughters, just as ignorant, just as unmindful of all the truths and hopes they have brought to America. They see daughters who grow impatient when their mothers talk in Chinese, who think they are stupid when they explain things in broken English. They see that joy and luck do not mean the same to their daughters, that to these American-born minds 'joy luck' does not exist.

'I will tell them everything,' I say simply, and the aunties look at me with doubtful faces. 'I will remember everything about her and tell them,' I say more firmly, and gradually, one by one, they smile, hopeful that what I say will become true. What more can they ask? What more can I promise?

They go back to telling stories among themselves. They are young girls again, dreaming of good times in the past and good times yet to come.

And I am sitting at my mother's place at the mah jong table, on the East, where things begin.

Scar

When I was a young girl in China, my grandmother, Popo, told me my mother was a ghost. This did not mean my mother was dead. In those days, a ghost was anything we were forbidden to talk about. So I knew Popo wanted me to forget my mother, and that is how I came to remember nothing of her. The life that I knew began in uncle and auntie's large house in Ningpo, where I lived with Popo and my little brother.

But I often heard stories of a ghost who tried to take children away, especially little girls who were disobedient. Many times Popo said aloud to all who could hear that my brother and I were eggs laid by a stupid bird, two eggs that nobody wanted, not even good enough to crack over a rice dish. She said this so that the ghosts would not steal us away. So you see, to Popo we were very precious.

All my life, I was afraid of Popo. I became even more afraid when she grew sick. This was in 1923, when I was nine years old. Her illness had made her body swell up, her skin became soft and rotten, and she smelt bad. She would call me into her room with the terrible smell and tell me stories.

'An-mei,' she said, 'listen carefully.' And she told me stories I could not understand, like the one about a girl who refused to listen to her family. One day this bad girl shook her head so hard when refusing her auntie's simple request, that a little white ball fell from her ear, and out poured all her brains, as clear as chicken soup.

Just before Popo became so ill that she could no longer speak, she pulled me close and talked to me about my mother. 'Never say her name,' she warned. 'To say her name is to spit on your father's grave.'

The only father I knew was a big painting that hung in the hall. He was a large, unsmiling man, whose restless eyes followed me around the house. Popo said he watched me for any signs of disrespect. Sometimes, if I had been naughty, I would quickly walk by my father with a know-nothing look, and hide in a corner of my room, where he could not see my face.

One hot summer day, we all stood outside watching a funeral procession go by. We could see the large, heavy picture of the dead man being carried by his family and friends, but just as it passed our gate, it fell to the ground with a crash. My brother laughed, and Auntie smacked him.

Auntie told him he had no respect for ancestors or family, just like our mother. Auntie had a tongue like hungry scissors eating silk cloth. So when my brother gave her a sour look, she said our mother was so thoughtless that she had left in a big hurry, without paying respect to my father's grave and those of our ancestors. When my brother accused Auntie of frightening our mother away, Auntie shouted that our mother had married a man called Wu Tsing who already had a wife, two concubines, and other bad children.

And when my brother shouted that Auntie was a talking chicken without a head, she spat in his face.

'You throw strong words at me, but you are nothing,' she said. 'You are the son of a mother who has betrayed our ancestors. She is so beneath other people that even the devil must look down to see her.'

That is when I began to understand the stories Popo taught me, the lessons I had to learn for my mother. Now I could imagine my mother, a thoughtless woman who was happy to be free of Popo, her sad husband on the wall, and her two disobedient children. I felt unlucky that she was my mother, and unlucky that she had left us.

I was sitting at the top of the stairs when she arrived. I knew it was my mother, even though I could not remember seeing her before. My auntie did not call her by name or offer her tea. I tried to keep very still, but my heart felt like a bird trying to escape from a cage. My mother must have heard, because she looked up. And when she did, I saw my own face looking back at me. Eyes that stayed wide open and saw too much.

My mother went straight to Popo's bedside and murmured, 'Come back, stay here. Your daughter is back now.' Popo did not seem to understand. If her mind had been clear, she would have thrown my mother out of the room. With her pretty, pale

My heart felt like a bird trying to escape from a cage.

face, my mother appeared to float in the room like a ghost, as she put cool cloths on Popo's swollen body. I watched her carefully, yet it was her voice that confused me, a familiar sound from a forgotten dream.

When I returned to my room later that afternoon, she was there, waiting for me. And because Popo had told me not to say her name, I stood there silently. She took my hand and led me to the sofa, where we sat down together as though we did this every day. She began to brush my hair with long, sweeping movements.

'An-mei, you have been a good daughter?' she asked, smiling a secret look.

I put on my know-nothing face, but inside I was trembling.

'An-mei, you know who I am,' she said with a scolding sound in her voice.

She stopped brushing. And then I could feel her long smooth fingers searching under my chin, finding my scar. As she rubbed it, I became very still. And then her hand dropped and she began to cry, sounding so sad. And then I remembered the dream with my mother's voice.

I was four years old. My chin was just above the dinner table, and I could hear voices praising a steaming dark soup in a large pot on the table.

And then the talking stopped. Everyone turned to look at the door, where a woman stood. I was the only one who spoke.

'Ma,' I cried, but my auntie smacked my face. Now everyone was standing up and shouting. I heard my mother calling, 'An-mei! An-mei!' Above this noise rose Popo's voice.

'Who is this ghost? Not an honoured widow. Just a number three concubine. If you take your daughter, she will become like you. No face. Never able to lift up her head.'

Still my mother shouted for me to come. I could see her face across the table. Between us stood the soup pot on its heavy stand, rocking slowly from side to side. And then suddenly this dark boiling soup spilled forward and fell all over my neck, as though everyone's anger were pouring all over me.

This was the kind of pain so terrible that a little child should never remember it. But it is still in my skin's memory. I could not see because of all the tears that poured out to wash away the pain, but I could hear my mother's crying. Popo and Auntie were shouting. And then my mother's voice went away.

Later that night Popo's voice came to me.

'An-mei, listen carefully. We have made your dying clothes for you.'

I listened, frightened.

'An-mei, if you die, you will still owe your family a debt.' And then Popo said something that was worse than the burning on my neck. 'Even your mother has used up her tears and left. If you do not get well soon, she will forget you.'

Popo was very smart. I came hurrying back from the other world to find my mother.

Every day a little skin came off, so that, in two years' time, my scar was pale and shiny, and I had no memory of my mother. That is the way it is with a wound. The wound begins to close in on itself, to protect what is hurting so much. And once it is closed, you no longer see what is underneath, what started the pain.

The feeling a daughter has for her mother is so deep that it is in her bones. Pain is nothing. Pain you must forget. Because sometimes that is the only way to remember what is in your bones. You have to get beneath your skin, and that of your mother, and her mother before her. Until there is nothing. No scar, no skin, just bones.

The Red Candle

I once sacrificed my life to keep my parents' promise. This means nothing to you, Waverly, because to you promises mean nothing. A daughter can promise to come to dinner, but if she has a headache, if she is in a traffic jam, if she wants to watch a favorite movie on TV, she no longer has a promise.

I watched this same movie when you did not come. The American soldier promises to come back and marry the girl. She is crying and he says, 'I promise! Sweetheart, my promise is as good as gold.' Then he pushes her onto the bed. But he doesn't come back. His gold is like yours, it is only fourteen carats.

To Chinese people, fourteen carats isn't real gold. Feel my bracelets. They must be twenty-four carats, pure inside and out.

It's too late to change you, but I'm telling you this because I worry about your baby. Some day she may say, 'Thank you, Grandmother, for the gold bracelet. I'll never forget you.' But later she will forget her promise. She will forget she had a grandmother.

In that same movie the American asks another girl to marry him. She loves him, so she says, 'Yes,' and they marry forever.

This did not happen to me. Instead, the village matchmaker came to my family when I was just two years old. With her was Huang Taitai, the mother of the boy I would be forced to marry. The matchmaker boasted about me and persuaded Huang Taitai that I would grow up to be a hard worker. That is how I became engaged to Tyan-yu, who I later discovered was just a baby, one year younger than me, and a spoilt, selfish child. But even if I had known I was getting such a bad husband, I had no choice. Mothers in country families always chose their sons' wives, ones who would bring up sons properly, care for the old people, and faithfully sweep the family burial grounds.

I didn't see my future husband until I was eight or nine, when I noticed him at one of the village ceremonies. He was a fat, babyish boy with a sour look on his face. So I didn't have instant love for him the way you see on television today. I thought of him as an annoying cousin, but I had to learn to be polite to the Huangs and especially to Huang Taitai.

My life changed completely when I was twelve, the summer the heavy rains came. The river which ran through my family's small farm flooded our fields. It destroyed everything we had planted that year and made the land useless for years to come. Even our house became uninhabitable, and we were suddenly very poor. So my father said we had no choice but to move to the south near Shanghai, where my mother's brother had a small business. My father explained that the whole family, except me, would leave immediately. I was old enough to separate from my family and go to live with the Huangs.

Before she left, my mother gave me her most valued necklace. As she put it round my neck, she looked very stern, so I knew she was very sad. 'Obey your family. Do not dishonour us,' she said. 'Act happy when you arrive. Really, you're very lucky.'

The Huangs' house had been untouched by the floods, as it was higher up the valley. I realized they had a much better position than my family, which is why they looked down on us. Their house was large enough for all the Huang great-grandparents, grandparents, parents, children and their servants, and looked important from the outside. Inside, there was a different kind of pretense. The only nice room was a sitting room on the first floor, which was used for receiving guests. It contained many precious things that gave the impression of wealth and ancient tradition. The rest of the house was plain and uncomfortable and noisy with the complaints of twenty or more relations.

No big celebration was held when I arrived. My future husband was not there to greet me. Instead, Huang Taitai hurried me into the kitchen, a place for cooks and servants. So I knew where I belonged. As I stood at the kitchen table on that first day, cutting up vegetables, I missed my family. But I was also determined to respect my parents' words, so that Huang Taitai could never accuse my mother of losing face.

I saw Tyan-yu at the evening meal. I knew what kind of husband he would be, because he made special efforts to make me cry, by complaining about my cooking and criticizing my appearance.

Over the next few years I was trained by Huang Taitai to sew, clean and cook to perfection. 'How can a wife keep house for her husband if she has never dirtied her own hands?' Huang Taitai used to say as she introduced me to a new skill. I don't think *she* ever dirtied her hands, but she was very good at calling out orders and criticizing. I was kept busy all day long. That was how I learnt to be an obedient wife.

After a while I didn't think it was a terrible life, no, not really. Can you see how the Huangs almost washed their thinking into my skin? I came to think of Tyan-yu as a god, someone whose opinions were worth much more than my own life. I came to think of Huang Taitai as my real mother, someone I wanted to please, someone I should follow and obey without question.

When I became sixteen, Huang Taitai told me she was ready to welcome a grandson by next spring. She started making preparations for our wedding, and invited family and friends from other cities, as well as the whole village.

But a lot of bad luck fell on our wedding day. The Japanese had invaded the neighbouring area the week before, and local people were nervous. On the day itself, rain began to fall, which was a very bad sign. When the thunder and lightning began, people confused it with Japanese bombs, and would not leave their houses. I heard later that poor Huang Taitai waited many hours for more guests to come. But finally she had to start the ceremony.

I was waiting in an upstairs room, crying and thinking bitterly about my parents' promise. What had I done to deserve such an unhappy life? From my seat by the window I could see the river, and I wondered whether to throw myself into the muddy brown waters that had destroyed my family's happiness.

And then I saw the curtains blowing wildly, and I heard the rain falling heavily, making people outside hurry and shout. I smiled, realizing it was the first time I could see the power of the wind. I wiped my eyes and looked in the mirror. I had on a beautiful red dress, but what I saw was even more valuable. I was strong. I was pure. I had real thoughts that no one could see, that no one could ever take away from me. I was like the wind.

And then I put the large red wedding scarf over my face and covered these thoughts up. But under the scarf I knew who I was. I promised myself I would always remember my parents' wishes, but I would never forget myself.

During the wedding ceremony the matchmaker held up a red candle for the handful of guests to see. It had two ends for lighting, one for Tyan-yu's name and the other for mine. She lit both ends and announced, 'The marriage has begun.'

She then handed the candle to a nervous-looking servant, who was supposed to watch it during the wedding dinner and all night, to make sure neither end went out. In the morning the matchmaker was supposed to show the blackened remains, and then declare, 'This candle burned continuously at both ends without going out. This is a marriage that can never be broken.'

It would mean I couldn't divorce and I couldn't remarry, even if Tyan-yu died. That red candle was supposed to tie me forever to my husband and his family, no excuses afterward.

And sure enough, the matchmaker made her declaration the next morning. But I know what really happened, because I stayed up all night crying about my marriage.

After the wedding dinner, people half-carried Tyan-yu and me up to our small bedroom, laughing and shouting jokes. But quite soon they left, and we sat side by side on the bed without speaking.

When the house grew quiet, Tyan-yu said, 'This is my bed. You sleep on the sofa.'

I was so glad. I waited until he fell asleep, then walked quietly downstairs into the courtyard.

Through a yellow-lit open window I could see the matchmaker's servant. She was sitting at a table, looking very sleepy as the red candle burned in front of her. I sat down by a tree to watch my future being decided for me.

I must have fallen asleep, because I was suddenly woken by the sound of loud cracking thunder. I saw the matchmaker's servant run from the room in terror. I laughed. She must have thought the thunder was a Japanese bomb, I said to myself. And then I saw the candle flame trembling in the wind. My legs lifted me up and ran me across the courtyard to get closer to the window. I was hoping and praying the candle would go out. My throat filled with so much hope that it finally burst and blew out my husband's end of the candle.

I was hoping and praying the candle would go out.

I shook with fear. I thought the sky would open up and blow me away. But nothing happened, and I walked back to my room with fast, guilty steps.

The next morning the matchmaker made her proud declaration in front of Tyan-yu and his family. 'My job is done,' she announced. I saw her servant's ashamed, miserable look.

From the beginning I felt sick thinking Tyan-yu would one day climb on top of me and do his business. But in the first months he never touched me. He slept in his bed, I slept on my sofa.

Even though I showed myself an obedient wife and did everything I could to please Huang Taitai, it was not enough to keep her happy. She soon realized Tyan-yu and I were not sleeping together, and blamed me for refusing him.

I knew I had to obey her, so one night I forced myself to share Tyan-yu's bed. He was frightened, and turned his head away. That's when I came to understand him. He had no desire for me, but it was his fear that made me realize he had no desire for any woman. After a while I was no longer afraid of him, and even began to love him, the way a sister loves a younger brother.

But Huang Taitai became angrier and angrier as the months passed and my stomach stayed flat. She kept me in bed all day, telling me to concentrate and think of nothing but having babies. Four times a day a very nice servant girl would bring me a terrible-tasting medicine. I envied this girl and her freedom to walk out of the door. Sometimes I watched her in the courtyard, laughing with other girls and scolding a handsome delivery man.

Then I thought of a plan. It was really quite simple. I would make the Huangs think it was their idea to get rid of me, so they would be the ones to say the marriage contract should be broken. I chose an important day, the Festival of Pure Brightness, when people think about their ancestors and visit the family graves. It has a special meaning to someone looking for grandsons.

On the morning of that day I woke Tyan-yu and the whole house with my screaming and crying. Huang Taitai rushed into my room, scolding me loudly. I had one hand over my mouth and the other over my eyes. I must have been convincing, because she drew back and grew small like a frightened animal.

'What's wrong, little daughter? Tell me quickly,' she said.

'Oh, it's too terrible to think, too terrible to say!' I gasped.

After enough crying, I said what was so unthinkable. 'I had a dream. Our ancestors came to me and said they wanted to see our wedding. So Tyan-yu and I showed our ancestors the ceremony. We saw the matchmaker light the candle and give it to her servant to watch . . .'

Huang Taitai began to look impatient as I began to cry again. 'But then the servant left the room and a big wind came and blew Tyan-yu's end of the candle out! And our ancestors said Tyan-yu would die if he stayed in this marriage!'

Tyan-yu's face turned white, but Huang Taitai only frowned. 'What a stupid girl to have such bad dreams!' she said.

'Mother,' I said sadly, 'they knew you would not believe me, because they know I do not want to leave the comforts of my marriage. So our ancestors said they would plant three signs, to show that our marriage is now rotten.'

'What nonsense from your stupid head!' said Huang Taitai. But she could not resist asking, 'What signs?'

'First, they have drawn a round black mark on Tyan-yu's back, which will grow and eat him up.'

Huang Taitai quickly turned to Tyan-yu and pulled his shirt up.

'Ai-ya!' she cried, because there it was, the same dark mark I had seen in these past five months of sleeping next to him.

'And then our ancestors touched my mouth,' I continued. 'They said my teeth would start to fall out one by one.'

Huang Taitai pulled open my mouth, and gasped upon seeing the space at the back, where a rotten tooth fell out four years ago.

'And finally they planted a seed in a servant girl. They said she is really of noble blood . . .' I lay back, as if too tired to go on.

Huang Taitai pushed my shoulder. 'What did they say?'

'They said the servant girl is Tyan-yu's true wife, and the seed they have planted will grow into Tyan-yu's child.'

By mid-morning they had forced the matchmaker's servant to make her terrible confession. And after a while they found the servant girl I liked so much, the one I had watched from my window. I had noticed her eyes grow bigger whenever the handsome delivery man arrived. Later, I had seen her stomach grow rounder and her face become longer with fear and worry. So you can imagine how happy she was when they made her tell the truth about her high-born ancestors, and marry Tyan-yu.

They didn't blame me so much. Huang Taitai got her grandson. I got my clothes, a rail ticket to Peking, and enough money to go to America.

It's a true story, how I kept my promise to my parents, how I sacrificed my life. Every few years, when I have a little extra money, I buy another bracelet. I know what I'm worth. They're always pure gold, twenty-four carats. But I'll always remember the day when I finally recognized a real thought and could follow where it went. That was the day I was a young girl with my face hidden under a red marriage scarf.

The Moon Lady

For all these years I kept my mouth closed, so selfish desires would not fall out. And because I remained quiet for so long, now my daughter does not hear me. She sits by her expensive swimming pool, and hears only her music, her phone, her big, important husband asking her why they have whiskey but no ice.

All these years I kept my true nature hidden, running along like a small shadow so nobody could catch me. And because I moved so secretly, now my daughter does not see me. She sees a list of things to buy, her checkbook out of balance, her magazine lying untidily on a chair.

And I want to tell her this: we are lost, she and I, unseen and not seeing, unheard and not hearing, unknown by others.

I did not lose myself all at once. My face disappeared over the years as I washed away my pain, just as stone is worn down by water. But today I can remember a time when I ran and shouted, when I could not stand still. It is my earliest memory: telling the Moon Lady my secret wish. And because I forgot what I wished for, that memory remained hidden from me all these many years. But now I remember the wish, and the details of that whole day, as clearly as I see my daughter and the foolishness of her life.

In 1918, when I was four years old, the Moon Festival arrived during an autumn in Wushi that was unusually hot. My amah appeared next to my bed the moment I woke up.

'No time to play today,' she said. 'Your mother has made you new clothes for the Moon Festival. It is a very important day, and now you are a big girl, you can go to the ceremony.'

As she helped me to put on the beautifully sewn silk jacket and skirt, I heard voices in the courtyard. Many relations from the north had arrived for the festival and were staying in our house for the week.

'We are all going to Tai Lake,' Amah went on. 'The family has rented a boat with a famous cook to prepare our dinner. And tonight at the ceremony you will see the Moon Lady.'

'The Moon Lady! The Moon Lady!' I shouted, jumping up and down in excitement. The news made me forget how hot I felt in the heavy new clothes. Then, no longer delighted by the sound of the unfamiliar words, I asked, 'Who is the Moon Lady?'

'Her name is Chang-o. She lives on the moon, and today is the only day you can see her and have your secret wish.'

'What is a secret wish?'

'It is what you want but cannot ask for,' said Amah.

'Why can't I ask for it?'

'Because . . . because if you ask . . . it is no longer a wish, but a selfish desire. Haven't I taught you that it is very wrong to think of your own needs? A girl can never ask, only listen.'

'Then how will the Moon Lady know my wish?'

'Ai! You ask too much already. You can ask her because she is not an ordinary person.'

Satisfied at last, I immediately said, 'Then I will tell her I don't want to wear these clothes any more.'

'Ah! Did I not just explain?' said Amah. 'Now that you have mentioned it to me, it is not a secret wish any more.'

During the morning meal nobody seemed in a hurry to go to the lake. The adults were always eating one more thing, or talking about matters of no importance. I grew more worried and unhappy by the minute, and sighed every time someone started a new conversation. Amah finally noticed me and gave me a sweet cake to eat. She told me to go and play in the courtyard with my two little half-sisters.

Outside I felt restless. Suddenly I saw a dragonfly with a large red body and transparent wings. I began to chase it, followed by my sisters. Just then my mother and the other ladies came into the courtyard.

'Ying-ying!' called Amah. She rushed towards me, and pulled my clothes straight. 'Everything all over the place!' she scolded.

My mother smiled and walked over to me. She stroked my untidy hair. 'A boy can run and chase dragonflies, because that is his nature,' she said. 'But a girl should stand still. If you are still for a very long time, a dragonfly will no longer see you. Then it will come to you and hide in the comfort of your shadow.' The old ladies murmured in agreement, and then they all left me in the middle of the hot courtyard.

Standing perfectly still like that, I discovered my shadow. When I shook my head, it shook its head. When I turned to walk away, it followed me. I screamed with delight at my shadow's own cleverness. I ran to the shade under the tree, watching my shadow chase me. It disappeared. I loved my shadow, this dark side of me that had my same restless nature.

And then it was time to go to the lake. The whole family was dressed in important-looking clothes, my father in expensive brown silk, Mama and I in yellow and black, my half-sisters and their mothers, my father's concubines, in rose pink. Even the old ladies had put on their best clothes to celebrate.

When we arrived at the lake, we climbed on board the large boat our family had rented. It looked like a floating teahouse. At first it was very exciting running from one end of the boat to the other, with unfamiliar sights and sounds all around me, as our boat moved slowly across the crowded lake. But soon the excitement faded, and the afternoon seemed to pass like any other at home. The same cold dishes for lunch. A little sleepy conversation, with hot tea. The quiet as everyone slept through the hottest part of the day.

When I woke up, I saw Amah was still asleep. I wandered round the boat by myself, and watched two rough-looking boys fishing from the back of the boat. When they stopped, I turned to see a cross-looking woman bending over a bucket of fish. Quickly and skillfully she cut open the fish, pulling out the red slippery insides and throwing them over her shoulder into the lake. I watched, fascinated, as she cut the heads off two chickens and threw the bodies into a pot. Then she carried everything, without a word, into the kitchen. And there was nothing else to see.

It was not until then, too late, that I saw my new clothes were covered in blood, bits of fish skin and feathers. When Amah found me, she called me names, using words I had never heard before, in a voice trembling not so much with anger as with fear. 'Evil, wicked one! Now your mother will be glad to get rid of you! She will send us both away!' Amah took my dirty clothes away, and left me standing in my white cotton underwear, crying bitterly.

I expected my mother to come and scold me in her gentle way. But she did not come. Once I heard someone approaching, but I saw only the faces of my half-sisters pressed to the door window. They looked at me wide-eyed, then laughed and ran off.

Now the water and the sky had darkened, and there were little red lights on the boats all over the lake. I was sitting on the edge of the boat, listening miserably to the happy sounds of people talking, laughing and eating all around me. In the dark water I could see the full moon, a moon so warm and big it looked like the sun. And I turned round so I could find the Moon Lady and tell her my secret wish. I fell into the water, not even hearing my own splash.

At first I was not afraid. I expected Amah to come immediately and pick me up. 'Amah!' I tried to cry. The sharp water rushed up my nose, into my throat and eyes. And then a dark shape wrapped round me and threw me into the air. I fell head first into a rope net full of fish.

I found myself on a small fishing boat, with four fishermen looking curiously down at me. They did not know which boat I had come from, and I could not tell them. All the boats looked the same to me, and I began to think I had lost my family forever. In the end they decided to put me down on the shore, and there I stood in the moonlight, quite alone except for my shadow.

I ran along the shore to where a crowd of people were standing. They were looking at a stage with a moon high up on it. A young man came on the stage and told the crowd, 'Now the Moon Lady will come and tell you her sad story.'

The Moon Lady! I thought, and the very sound of those magic words made me forget my troubles. The shadow of a woman appeared against the moon. She was combing her long straight hair and speaking in a sweet, sad voice. She spoke of her dearly loved husband, who lived far away from her on the sun. She described the fruit that her husband hid from her, because he hoped it would give him everlasting life, and she told us how she could not resist stealing it and eating it. Her husband's anger and her realization of her selfishness were not enough to punish her. She now had to stay on the moon, forever alone.

'For woman is *yin*,' she cried sadly, 'the darkness inside us, where uncontrolled passions lie. And man is *yang*, bright truth lighting our minds.'

At the end, I was crying with despair. She and I had both lost the world, and there was no way to get it back.

The young man came on stage again, and asked if, for a small fee, anyone wanted to ask the Moon Lady for a secret wish. The audience did not seem interested and started moving away, until only my shadow and I were left.

'I have a wish! I have one!' I shouted, but the young man had already left the stage. I ran round to the back, to the other side of the moon. There I saw the Moon Lady, looking beautiful in the lamplight, but she did not hear me when I called. So I walked closer, until I could see her face, with its wide nose, large yellow teeth, and red eyes. She pulled off her long hair, and her dress fell from her shoulders. And as the secret wish fell from my lips, the Moon Lady looked at me and became a man.

For many years, I could not remember what I wanted that night from the Moon Lady, or how it was that I was found again by my family. But now that I am old, moving every year closer to the end of my life, I also feel closer to the beginning. And I remember everything that happened that day because it has happened many times in my life. The same innocence, trust, and restlessness, the wonder, fear, and loneliness. How I lost myself.

I remember all these things. And tonight I also remember what I asked the Moon Lady so long ago. I wished to be found.

The Twenty-Six Malignant Gates

'DO NOT RIDE *your bicycle around the corner,*' *the mother had told the daughter when she was seven. 'Because then I cannot see you and you will fall down and cry and I will not hear you.'*

'How do you know I'll fall?' protested the girl.

'It is in a book, The Twenty-Six Malignant Gates, *all the bad things that can happen to you outside the protection of this house.'*

'I don't believe you. Let me see the book.'

'It is written in Chinese. You cannot understand it. That is why you must listen to me.'

'Tell me,' the girl demanded. 'Tell me these twenty-six bad things.'

But the mother sat sewing in silence.

'What twenty-six!' shouted the girl.

The mother still did not answer her.

'You can't tell me because you don't know! You don't know anything!' And the girl ran outside, jumped on her bicycle, and in her hurry to get away, she fell before she even reached the corner.

American Translation

'WAH!' CRIED THE MOTHER, *seeing the mirror in the bedroom of her daughter's new apartment. 'You cannot put mirrors at the foot of the bed. All your marriage happiness will jump back and turn the opposite way.'*

'That's the only place where it can go,' said the daughter, annoyed that her mother saw bad omens in everything. She had heard these warnings all her life.

'Hnnh, lucky I can fix it for you, then.' And the mother took out the little mirror she had bought as a housewarming present.

'Hang it up there,' she said, pointing to the wall above the bed. 'This mirror sees that mirror. It will increase your peach-blossom luck.'

'What is peach-blossom luck?'

The mother smiled. 'It is in here,' she said, pointing to the mirror. 'Look inside. In this mirror is my future grandchild, lying in my arms next spring.'

And the daughter looked – and there it was: her own reflection looking back at her.

Rules of the Game

I was six when my mother taught me how to have invisible strength. It was a way of winning arguments, respect from others, and eventually, though neither of us knew it then, chess games.

'Bite back your tongue,' scolded my mother when I cried loudly for the delicious salted fruit at our local shop. At home, she said, 'Wise man, he not go against wind. Strongest wind cannot be seen.'

The next week I bit back my tongue as we entered the shop. When my mother had finished her shopping, she quietly took a bag of fruit from the shelf, paid for it, and handed it to me.

We lived in a two-bedroom flat in San Francisco's Chinatown, above a Chinese baker's shop in Waverly Place. My mother named me after this street. Like most of the other Chinese children who played in the back streets of restaurants and tourist shops, I didn't think we were poor. My bowl was always full, and we had three large meals a day.

My oldest brother Vincent was the one who actually got the chess set. We had gone to the Christmas party held by the local church, and the kindly, grey-haired ladies had put together a bag of presents for us children. When Vincent got the chess set, my mother bowed and thanked the unknown giver, saying, 'Too good. Cost too much.' An old lady with fine white hair nodded towards our family, and said with a whistling whisper, 'Happy, happy Christmas.'

When we arrived home, my mother told Vincent to throw the

chess set away. 'She not want it. We not want it,' she said, throwing her head stiffly to one side with a tight, proud smile. My brothers had deaf ears. They were already lining up the chessmen and reading from the well-worn instruction book.

I watched my brothers play during the whole of that week. The game seemed to hold dark secrets, just waiting to be discovered. They finally agreed to let me play, and Vincent read out the rules to me. Later I read them for myself, and looked up all the big words in a dictionary. I borrowed books on chess from the Chinatown library, and studied each chess piece, trying to find the power it contained. I drew a chessboard and put it on the wall next to my bed, where at night I would stare for hours at imaginary battles on those sixty-four black and white squares.

Soon I no longer lost any games, but my brothers lost interest in playing. Fortunately, we had a neighbour, Lau Po, who was an experienced player, and over the weeks he taught me everything he knew. From him I learnt the secret moves, including their names: The Double Attack from the East and West Shores, Throwing Stones on the Drowning Man, The Sudden Meeting of the Family, The Surprise from the Sleeping Guard, The Servant Who Kills the King, Sand in the Eyes of the Advancing Enemy, A Double Killing Without Blood.

It wasn't long before I was playing in official matches. My mother always came with me, sitting proudly beside me and telling my admirers, with proper Chinese modesty, 'Is luck, that's all.'

When I played, I didn't see the person sitting opposite me, I only saw the black and white chessmen on the board. A light wind blew past my ears, whispering secrets only I could hear. 'Blow from the south,' it murmured, or, 'throw sand from the east to confuse him.' And when I won, the wind shouted with laughter and then died down, to become my own breath.

By my ninth birthday, I was a national chess champion, and people said I had a great future as an international player. My mother decided I did not have to help with the housework any more, although my brothers protested bitterly at this. But there was one duty I couldn't avoid. When I had no match to play, I had to go shopping with my mother on Saturday market days. She would walk proudly with me, visiting many shops, buying very little. 'This my daughter Waverly Jong,' she said to whoever looked in her direction.

One day, after we had left a shop, I whispered, 'I wish you wouldn't tell everyone I'm your daughter.' My mother stopped walking. Crowds of people with heavy bags pushed past us.

'Aii-ya. So shame be with mother?' She held my hand even more tightly as she stared angrily at me.

'It's not that. It's just so embarrassing.'

'Embarrass you be my daughter?' Her voice was cracking with anger.

'That's not what I meant. That's not what I said.'

'What you say?'

I knew it was a mistake to say anything more, but I heard my voice speaking. 'Why do you have to use me to show off? If you want to show off, then why don't you learn to play chess?'

My mother's eyes turned into dangerous black holes. She had no words for me, just sharp silence. I felt the wind rushing round my hot ears. I pulled my hand out of hers and spun round, knocking into an old woman, who dropped her bag of shopping.

'Aii-ya! Stupid girl!' my mother and the old woman cried. As my mother bent to help the old woman pick up her vegetables, I ran off down the street.

I ran and ran, until I realized I had nowhere to go. My breath came out like angry smoke. It was cold. I sat down on an

I pulled my hand out of hers and spun round.

upturned bucket, imagining my mother searching and calling for me. After two hours, I stood up and slowly walked home.

I could see the yellow lights shining from our flat like two tiger's eyes in the night. I crept up the steps to the door and quietly turned the handle. The door was locked. I heard a chair move inside, the locks turned, and then the door opened.

'About time you got home,' said Vincent. 'Wow, you really are in trouble.'

He went back to the dinner table. Standing there waiting for my punishment, I heard my mother speak in a dry voice.

'We not concerned with this girl. This girl not concerned with us.'

Nobody looked at me. Bone chopsticks knocked against the sides of bowls being emptied into hungry mouths.

I walked into my room, closed the door, and lay down on my bed in the dark. In my head I saw a chessboard. The player opposite me had eyes like angry black holes in her face. She wore a proud smile. 'Strongest wind cannot be seen,' she said.

Her black chessmen advanced, and my white pieces screamed as they fell off the board one by one. I felt myself growing light. I rose up into the air and flew out of the window, carried by the wind. Then everything below me disappeared, and I was alone.

I closed my eyes and thought about my next move.

Many years later, when I was in a well-paid job, with my own life, my own home, I still tried to plan my moves in the long-running battle with my mother. On this occasion I had taken her out to lunch at my favorite Chinese restaurant, in the hope of putting her in a good mood, but it was a disaster. She disapproved of my new haircut, criticized the menu, and complained to the waiter that the chopsticks were dirty. Her soup was not hot enough, and her tea was too expensive.

'You shouldn't get so upset,' I told her. 'Bad for your heart.'

'Nothing is wrong with my heart,' she replied sharply.

And she was right. Despite all the worry she gives herself – and others – the doctors say that my mother, at sixty-nine, has the heart of a sixteen-year-old and the strength of a horse. And that's what she is, according to the Chinese calendar, a Horse, born in 1918, bound to speak her mind in every situation. She and I make a bad combination, because I'm a Rabbit, born in 1951, supposedly sensitive, especially when criticized.

After our miserable lunch, I gave up the idea that there would ever be a good time to tell her the news: that Rich Schields and I were getting married. My mother had never met Rich. In fact, whenever I mentioned him, she always thought of something else to talk about. So I decided to make her become aware of his place in my life, by taking her back to my apartment after lunch. She had not been there for months. When I was married to my first husband, she used to arrive with no warning, until one day I suggested she should phone in advance. Ever since then, she has refused to come unless I give her an official invitation.

So I watched her as she inspected my untidy home, a place full of love and life. The beds were unmade, my four-year-old daughter Shoshana's toys were all over the floor, and Rich's clothes lay over the backs of chairs. My mother picked her way through the mess, a look of distaste on her face. How could she *not* notice that we were living together?

From the wardrobe I took a real fur jacket that Rich had given me for Christmas. It was the most expensive present I had ever received. I put it on, to show my mother.

She was quiet. She ran her fingers over the fur. 'This is not so good,' she said at last. 'Is just small pieces. Fur is too short.'

'How can you criticize a gift!' I protested. I was deeply wounded. 'He gave me this from his heart.'

'That is why I worry,' she said.

And, when I looked at the coat in the mirror, I couldn't resist the force of her opinion, her ability to make me see black where there was once white. Now the coat seemed of poor quality, an imitation of love and affection.

'Aren't you going to say anything else?' I asked softly. 'About all *this*?' I pointed to the signs of Rich lying about.

She looked round the room, and finally she said, 'You have job. You are busy. You want to live like mess what I can say?'

My mother knows how to hurt me. And the pain I feel is worse than any other kind of misery. Because what she does always comes as a shock, which digs itself permanently into my memory. I still remember the first time I felt it.

I was ten years old. Even though I was young, I knew my skill at playing chess was a gift. It was effortless, so easy. I could see things on the chessboard that other people could not. And this gift gave me a wonderful confidence. I loved to win.

And my mother loved to show me off. She used to discuss my games as if she had planned how to win them, and to our family friends she would explain, 'You don't have to be smart to win chess. It's just tricks. You blow from the north, south, east and west. Then other person becomes confused.'

I hated the way she pretended that she, not I, was the expert. And one Saturday morning I told her so, in the middle of a crowd of people at the market. That day and the next, she refused to speak to me, as if I had become invisible, and *I* wouldn't speak to *her*.

Many days passed by in silence, and I sat in my room, trying to think of another plan. That's when I decided to give up chess.

Of course, I didn't intend to stop for ever. I thought she would come to me, crying, 'Why are you not playing?' But nothing happened. She said nothing, and I was crying inside, because I was missing several important matches. I realized she knew more tricks than I thought. But I was tired of her game. So I decided to pretend to let her win.

'I am ready to play chess again,' I announced to her one day. I imagined she would smile and ask me what special thing I would like to eat.

But instead, she frowned at me. 'You think it is so easy,' she said. 'One day stop, next day play. Everything for you is this way. So smart, so easy, so fast.'

'I said I'll play,' I said, beginning to cry.

'No!' she shouted. It was so sudden it made me jump. 'It is not so easy any more.'

I could not understand what was happening. But I did win my mother back. That night I developed a high fever, and she sat next to my bed, feeding me with chicken soup and rice. But after I got well, I discovered that she had changed. She no longer watched over me as I practiced, or boasted of my achievements. And when I lost my next match, she said nothing. She almost seemed satisfied, as if she had planned it.

I was horrified, and spent many hours going over the moves in my mind. I realized I could no longer see the secret weapons of each chessman, or the magic in every square.

Over the next few years I continued to play, but I had lost that feeling of confidence. When I won, I was relieved. And when I lost, I was filled with growing fear that I no longer had the gift, and was becoming just an ordinary person. When I was fourteen, I stopped playing chess completely. And nobody protested.

I told a friend what my mother had said about the fur coat Rich had given me, but she couldn't understand my problem. 'You can tell a tax officer to go to hell,' she said, 'but you can't deal with your own mother. Tell her to shut up, stop ruining your life.'

But this time I wasn't so much afraid of my mother as I was afraid for Rich. I already knew how she would attack and criticize him. And I was afraid that some of the unseen dust of truth would fly into my eye, confuse what I was seeing, and change him from the wonderful man I thought he was, into someone quite ordinary, with annoying habits and faults.

This had happened to my first marriage, to Marvin Chen. When I was in love with Marvin, he was almost perfect, but by the time my mother had had her say about him, I realized he was lazy, selfish and mean. It wasn't until after we separated, on nights when Shoshana was asleep and I was lonely, that I wondered if perhaps my mother had poisoned my marriage.

And now I worried for Rich. Because I knew my feelings for him could be damaged by my mother's comments. And I was afraid of what I would then lose, because Rich loved me in the same way I loved Shoshana. Nothing could change it. He expected nothing from me; just the fact that I existed was enough for him. I'd never known love so pure, and I was afraid it would become dirtied by my mother.

I managed to persuade my mother to invite Rich, Shoshana and me over for a meal. Cooking was the way my mother expressed her love, her pride and her power, and I hoped this would soften her when she met Rich for the first time.

Before we arrived, I tried to prepare Rich, by telling him he must praise her food. But Rich was not Chinese, and there were so many other things he did not know about, so many mistakes he could make. I could not save him from all of them.

So, during the meal, Rich followed American rules of politeness, without having any idea how strange they seemed to my parents. Not only did he drop most of his food on his trousers because he insisted on using chopsticks, he also refused a second serving. He should have followed my father's example, and taken a third, or even a fourth. But what was worse, he failed to contradict my mother's modest statement that a particular dish lacked flavour; he thought it was polite to agree, but, in her eyes, nothing could be ruder. I knew she would not have a good word to say about him. Sure enough, when I was in the kitchen helping her to clear away the dishes, she found fault with his appearance, his habits and even his character. There was nothing I could do.

That night, I lay in bed, despairing over this latest failure. And Rich seemed blind to it all! He thought the dinner had gone well. I began to see him from my mother's point of view – weak, not strong, insensitive, not caring. My mother was doing it again, making me see black where I once saw white.

The next morning I woke up late, feeling furious with my mother. Without speaking to Rich, I jumped in the car and drove to my parents' apartment. I found my mother sleeping on the sofa in the living room. With her smooth, innocent face, she looked like a young girl again. All her strength was gone. She had no weapons. She looked powerless, defeated.

And then I had a sudden fear that she looked like this because she was dead. She had died while I was having terrible thoughts about her. I had wished her out of my life.

'Ma!' I said sharply. 'Ma!' I was starting to cry.

Slowly she opened her eyes and sat up. 'What has happened?' she asked. 'Why are you crying?'

I felt confused. In a few seconds I had gone from anger to pity to fear, and now I felt strangely weak. 'Nothing's happened,' I said. 'I wanted to talk to you . . . to tell you . . . Rich and I are getting married.'

I waited to hear her protests, her dry remarks.

'Of course I know this,' she said.

This was worse than I had imagined. She had known all the time! 'I know you hate him,' I said in a shaking voice, 'but—'

'Hate? Why do you think I hate your future husband?'

'You – you never want to hear about him. And then you – you criticize him, just to hurt me . . .'

'Aii-ya, why do you think these bad things about me?' Her face looked old and full of sorrow. 'Aii-ya! She thinks I am this bad!' She sat straight and proud on the sofa, her mouth held tightly shut, and her eyes shining with angry tears.

Oh, her strength! her weakness! Both were pulling me apart. My mind was flying one way, my heart another. I sat down beside her and we went on talking.

And gradually I realized what I had done. I had built an invisible wall between us, to protect myself from what I saw as her secret weapons, her skill at finding my weaknesses. But now a door in the wall had opened, and I could finally see what was really there: an old woman, getting a little bad-tempered as she waited patiently for her daughter to invite her in.

We have decided to postpone our wedding. My mother tells Rich that July is not a good time to go to China on our wedding trip.

'Too hot. Your whole face will become red,' she says, and Rich laughs.

If we go in October, I think she would love to come with us. And I would hate it. Three weeks of her constant complaints about dirty chopsticks and cold soup.

Yet part of me also thinks the whole idea makes perfect sense. The three of us, leaving our differences behind, stepping on the plane together, sitting side by side, moving west to reach the east.

LENA ST CLAIR
Daughter of Ying-ying St Clair

The Voice from the Wall

All my life I have thought it was important to know the worst possible thing that can happen to you, so you can find out how to avoid it. Because, even as a young child, I could sense the unspoken terrors that surrounded our house, the ones that chased my mother until she hid in a secret, dark corner of her mind. And still they found her. I watched, over the years, as they ate her up, piece by piece, until she disappeared and became a ghost.

As I remember it, the dark side of my mother came from the basement of our house. I was five, and she tried to hide it from me. She put two locks and a chain on the door, and pushed a heavy chair against it. But this made it so mysterious that I spent all my energies trying to get in, until the day I finally managed to open the door, only to fall head first into the dark space. And it was only after I stopped screaming that my mother told me about the bad man who lived in the basement, and why I should never open the door again. He had lived there for thousands of years, she said, and was so evil and hungry that if she had not rescued me so quickly, he would have planted five babies in me, and then eaten us all, throwing our bones on the dirty floor.

After that I began to see terrible things. Devils dancing in a hole I had dug in the sand, lightning with eyes that searched for little children to strike, an insect wearing the face of a child. I saw these things with my Chinese eyes, the part of me I got from my mother. Most people didn't know I was half Chinese. When they first saw me, they thought I looked like my father, English-Irish.

But if they looked closely, they could see the Chinese parts, the smooth bones of my face and the long shape of my eyes. I used to open my eyes very wide to make them look rounder, but then my father always asked me why I looked so afraid.

I have a photo of my mother with this same frightened look. My father had married her in China and brought her to America with him, so the picture was taken when she first arrived in America as a new bride. She never talked about her life in China, but my father said he had saved her from a terrible life there. In the photo her eyes are staring up past the camera, wide open. She often looked like this, waiting for something to happen. Only later she lost the struggle to keep her eyes open.

My father, who only knew a few Chinese expressions, had insisted my mother should learn English. So with him, she spoke in moods and sign language, looks and silences, a combination of English and Chinese. Then he would put words in her mouth.

'I think Mom is trying to say she's tired,' he would whisper to me when she became moody.

But with me, when we were alone, my mother would speak Chinese, saying things that my father could not possibly imagine, and that I had difficulty understanding.

'You must not walk in any direction but to school and back home,' she warned, when she had decided I was old enough to walk by myself.

'Why?' I asked.

'You can't understand these things,' she said.

'Why not?'

'Because I haven't put it in your mind yet.'

'Why not?'

'Aii-ya! Such questions! Because it is too terrible to consider. A man can steal you off the street, sell you to someone else, make you have a baby. Then you'll kill the baby. And when the police find this baby, you'll go to prison and die there.'

I knew this was not a true answer. It was her way of warning me, to help me avoid all danger, now and in the future.

When I was ten, we moved house, to a block of flats on a steep hill. I hoped we could leave all the old fears behind. But my mother did not seem happy with our new apartment, and every day she rearranged the furniture.

'Why are you doing this?' I asked one day.

'When something goes against your nature,' she whispered worriedly, 'you are not in balance. This apartment block was built too steep, and a bad wind from the top blows all your strength back downhill. So you can never make progress.'

My father just smiled when I asked him about it, and explained that she was expecting a baby. He seemed to think it was quite normal behaviour. I wondered why he never worried. Was he blind? My mother did not speak of the joys of having a new baby, but talked of a heaviness around her, a lack of balance. It made me feel very anxious.

My mother had changed my bedroom round to make room for the baby's bed, and now my bed was right next to the thin wall that divided us from our neighbours' flat. I knew that a family called the Sorcis lived there.

The first night I could hear a heated argument going on. First I heard a woman's angry voice, then the higher sound of a girl shouting back. I could hear accusations and protests, and then a terrible crashing and banging, and the sound of a violent beating. Someone was killing. Someone was being killed.

I lay back, my heart beating wildly at what my ears and imagination had just witnessed. A girl had just been killed, and I hadn't been able to prevent it. The horror of it all!

But the next night, the girl came back to life with more screams, more beatings, her life once more in danger. And so it continued, night after night, a voice behind my wall telling me that this was the worst possible thing that could happen: the terror of not knowing when it would ever stop.

When I saw the girl coming out of the flat one morning, I was amazed to see that she looked healthy and cheerful. She didn't seem like a girl who had been killed a hundred times. I kept out of her way, feeling guilty that I knew all about her family life.

One day my parents' friends Auntie Suyuan and Uncle Canning picked me up from school and took me to the hospital to see my mother. I knew it must be serious, and when we arrived, I found my father sitting by my mother's bedside, looking desperately worried. She held my hand, her whole body shaking, and murmured to me in Chinese.

'Lena, what's she saying?' cried my father. For once, he had no words to put in her mouth.

And for once, I had no ready answer. It struck me that the worst possible thing had happened, that what she had been fearing had come true. And so I listened.

'I could hear the baby screaming inside me,' whispered my mother. 'He didn't want to be born. But when he came, I saw at once he had a large head so terrible I could not stop staring at it. His head was open, so I could see all the way back to where his thoughts were supposed to be, and there was nothing there! And then this empty head rose up and looked at me. I knew he could see my thoughts – how I had not wanted this baby!'

I could not tell my father what she said. He was so sad already. How could I make it worse by telling him she was crazy? So I just said, 'She says she hopes the baby is very happy on the other side. And she thinks we should leave now.'

After the baby's death, my mother fell apart, not all at once, but piece by piece, like plates falling off a shelf one by one. She often had to stop what she was doing because she was crying so much, or holding her head in despair, or simply staring into the

'I could hear the baby screaming inside me,' whispered my mother.

distance with empty eyes. I became nervous, constantly waiting for something to happen, and I could feel every movement in our silent flat. And at night, I could hear the loud fights on the other side of my bedroom wall, where a girl was being beaten to death. I used to wonder which was worse, our side or theirs? And it made me feel better to think that, after all, the girl next door had a more unhappy life.

But one evening the doorbell rang, and when I went to the door, the girl from the other side of the wall came in. She smiled at me, then rushed past me towards my bedroom. I followed her in great surprise, and saw her opening the window.

'What are you doing?' I asked.

'My mother threw me out of the house.' She laughed. 'Now she thinks I'm going to go back and apologize. But I'm not!'

'So what *are* you going to do?' I asked breathlessly.

'I'm going to climb out of your window and back in through mine,' she replied. 'That way I won't have to wait outside in the cold until she unlocks the front door. She'll pretend to be angry with me, of course. We do this kind of thing all the time.'

And then she climbed through my window onto the fire escape staircase and silently made her way back home. I stared at the open window, wondering about her. How could she go back? Didn't she see how terrible her life was?

Late that night, I heard screams and shouts, as the mother discovered her daughter was back in her room. And then I heard them laughing and crying, shouting with love. I was amazed. I could almost see them holding and kissing each other. I was crying for joy with them, because I had been wrong.

And in my memory I can still feel the hope that was born in me that night. I held on to this hope night after night, year after year. I would watch my mother lying in bed, talking softly to herself.

But I knew that this, the worst possible thing, would one day stop. I still saw bad things in my mind, but I saw other things too.

I saw a girl complaining that the pain of not being seen was unbearable. I saw the mother lying in bed. Then the girl pulled out a sharp knife, and told her mother, 'You must die the death of a thousand cuts. It is the only way to save you.'

The mother accepted this and closed her eyes. The knife came down, and the mother screamed and cried out in terror and pain. But when she opened her eyes, she saw no blood.

The girl said, 'Do you see now?'

The mother nodded. 'Now I have already experienced the worst. After this, there is no worst possible thing.'

And the daughter said, 'Now you must come back, to the other side. Then you can see why you were wrong.' And the girl took her mother's hand and pulled her through the wall.

To this day, I believe that my mother has the mysterious ability to see things before they happen. She thought her baby would die, and it did. She knew that my father would die, at the age of seventy-four, because a plant he had given her had died. And now that she is visiting my husband and me in our new house, I wonder what kind of future she will see for us.

Harold and I were lucky to find this place, which is right out in the country, but only a forty-minute drive from San Francisco. My mother, however, cannot believe how much we paid for what was basically a farm building with some expensive additions. It annoys me that she only sees the disadvantages. But then I look around, and everything she has said is true.

And this convinces me she can see what else is going on, between Harold and me. Our problems are deep, so deep that I don't even know where bottom is. Now that my mother is staying with us for a week, we have to pretend that nothing is the matter. But I know she will see through our pretense.

I remember something else she saw, when I was eight years old. She had looked in my rice bowl and told me I would marry a bad man, a mean man with scars on his face, unless I finished up all my rice. I immediately thought of a twelve-year-old boy I knew, a cruel boy, a mean boy, whose face was covered with tiny scars. His name was Arnold. I didn't want him to be my future husband, so I ate up all my rice and smiled confidently at my mother.

But she only sighed and said, 'Yesterday, you not finish rice either.' I was shocked to think that I would be obliged to have a bad husband because of my poor eating habits.

Soon my dislike for Arnold grew to such hatred that I found a way to make him die. At school the teacher showed us a film of people in Africa suffering from the most terrible skin diseases. I knew that if my mother had been in the room, she would have told me that these poor people were victims of future husbands and wives who had failed to eat *platefuls* of food.

So I did an awful thing. I began to leave more rice in my bowl. I did not finish my vegetables, or chicken, or sandwiches. Perhaps as a result of my actions, Arnold would catch a skin disease, move to Africa and die. That was certainly my intention.

In fact, he didn't die until five years later. I had almost stopped eating by then, not because of Arnold, whom I had long forgotten, but in order to be fashionably thin like all the other thirteen-year-old girls. From the newspaper, my father read out the news of Arnold's death, caused by complications from an infection the boy had had when he was twelve.

'This is terrible shame,' said my mother, looking at me. I thought she could see through me, and that she knew I was the one who had made Arnold die. I was terrified. That evening I stole a huge pot of ice cream from the freezer, and forced myself to eat it all. I felt ill, and miserably unhappy, all night.

Of course, now I can see that I probably had nothing at all to do with Arnold's death. But I still believe that, somehow, we deserve what we get. I didn't get Arnold. I got Harold.

Harold and I work in the same company, only he is the boss and I am an employee. We met eight years ago, when we were both working for another company. We started seeing each other for working lunches, to talk about projects, and we always divided the bill equally, even though I usually only ordered a salad. Later, when we started spending evenings out together, we still divided the bill. And we just continued that way, sharing all the costs. I even encouraged it. It really didn't bother me.

Harold told me I was extraordinary. He had never met another woman who was so balanced, so organized and yet so lovable.

I remember wondering how such a remarkable person as Harold could think I was extraordinary. Now that I'm angry with him, it's hard to remember what was so remarkable about him, but at the time, I felt awfully lucky, and very worried that all this undeserved good luck might one day slip away.

But I knew I was smart. After all, it was my idea that he should start his own business designing restaurants. And when he did, I went to work for him. I was the one who gave him most of the ideas that have helped make his company so successful. I love my work when I don't think about it too much. And when I do think about it, how little I get paid, how hard I work, I get upset.

Harold has gone shopping, so my mother and I are alone in the house. She is looking at a piece of paper on the fridge door. It's a list of the different things Harold and I have paid for so far this week. At the end of the week, the one who has spent less pays the other one back.

'What is this writing?' asks my mother in Chinese.

'Oh nothing, really. Just things we share,' I say as casually as I can.

She looks at me, frowning. Knowing what she's seeing, I feel embarrassed. I'm relieved she doesn't see the other half of it, the endless discussions about who should pay for what.

'This you don't share!' cries my mother, pointing to 'ice cream' on the list. It is true I could never bear to eat it after the night I heard of Arnold's death. It comes as a shock to realize that Harold has never noticed I don't touch any of the ice cream he brings home every Friday evening.

'Why you do this?' asks my mother sadly.

'I don't really know. It's something we started before we got married. And for some reason we never stopped.'

After dinner I take my mother to the guest room. There is an odd-looking table by the bed, with a vase of flowers on it. She puts her handbag on the table, and the flowers tremble.

'Careful, it's not very strong,' I say. The table is a poorly designed piece, made by Harold in his student days. I've always wondered why he's so proud of it.

'What use for?' asks my mother. 'Not good balance.'

When I go downstairs, I am feeling furious with Harold. I go to the list on the fridge and cross out 'ice cream' under his name.

'What's going on here?' he asks.

'I just don't think you should make me pay for *your* ice cream any more.'

'What? You've decided you don't like ice cream now?'

'I've never liked it. I've hated ice cream almost all my life.'

Harold's mouth drops open.

After a while he says, 'I guess I assumed you were just trying to lose weight. Oh well.'

'Well, you were wrong!' I shout.

'What *is* this? Why don't you say what's really the matter?'

'I don't know. Everything. What we share. What we don't share. The way we put a price on everything. I'm so tired of it!'

I start to cry, which I know Harold hates. But I can't help it, because I realize now that I don't know why I started this argument. None of it seems right. None of it makes sense. I can admit to nothing and I am in complete despair.

'I just think we have to change things,' I say, when I can control my voice. 'We need to think about our relationship, not just who owes what.'

'My God,' says Harold, and sighs. Finally he says in a hurt voice, 'Well, I know our marriage is about a lot more than just paying the bills. And if you don't, then I think you should think carefully before you change things.'

And now I don't know what to think. What am I saying? What is he saying? We sit in the room in silence. And then I hear a crash from upstairs. 'I'll go and see,' I say.

The door is open, but the room is dark, so I call out, 'Ma?' The table lies on its side on the floor, with the broken pieces of the vase around it. My mother is sitting by the open window, a dark shape visible against the night sky. I can't see her face.

'Fallen down,' she says simply. She doesn't apologize.

'It doesn't matter,' I say, picking up the pieces. 'I knew it would happen.'

'Then why don't you stop it?' asks my mother.

And it's such a simple question.

Without Wood

As proof of her religious faith, my mother used to carry a small Bible when she went to church every Sunday, But later, after she lost her faith in God, that Bible ended up under a too-short table leg in our kitchen. It's been there for over twenty years. My mother pretends it isn't there, but I know she sees it.

Tonight I'm watching her sweep under the same kitchen table, around the Bible. I am waiting for the right moment to tell her that Ted and I are getting divorced.

When I tell her, I know she's going to say, 'This cannot be.' And when I reply that our marriage is certainly over, I know what else she will say: 'Then you must save it.'

And even though there's absolutely nothing left to save – I'm afraid if I tell her that, she'll still persuade me to try.

I think it's quite amusing that my mother wants me to fight the divorce. She didn't like it when I started going out with Ted Jordan, seventeen years ago, because he was American, not Chinese.

Ted's mother also had a few words to say about our relationship. The first time I met her, she took me aside to tell me about Ted's need to concentrate on his medical studies, and the fact that it would be years before he could even consider marrying. She also explained that, although she and her husband naturally had no prejudices themselves, Ted was going to be in an important profession, where he would be judged by patients and colleagues who might not be as understanding as the Jordans.

When I told Ted about this, it made him furious. 'Are you going to let my mother decide what's right?' he shouted. I was touched that he was so upset.

'What should we do?' I asked, and I had a pained feeling I thought was the beginning of love. Our parents' displeasure brought us closer together. Soon we were inseparable, two halves creating a whole: *yin* and *yang*. I was victim to his hero. I was weak; he protected me. I was in danger; he rescued me.

'What should we do?' I continued to ask him. And within a year of our first meeting, we were living together. As soon as Ted got his first job, we married and bought an old house with a large garden. I worked from home, as a designer.

Over the years, Ted made all the decisions. At first, we discussed things, but in the end I always said, 'Ted, you decide.' After a while, there were no more discussions. Ted simply decided. And I never thought of objecting.

But last year an operation on a patient went badly wrong, which cost Ted a lot of money and damaged his confidence. This made him change his feelings about what he called 'decision and responsibility'. He started pushing me to make decisions. Should we buy an American or Japanese car? Should we buy more shares? Who should we vote for? Should we start a family?

I thought about the advantages and disadvantages of these things. But in the end I was confused, because I never believed there was one right answer. So whenever I said, 'Either way is fine with me,' Ted would say impatiently, 'You can't have it both ways, none of the responsibility, none of the blame.'

Last month, when he was about to leave for a two-day business trip to Los Angeles, he asked if I wanted to go with him, and then quickly added, 'Never mind, I'd rather go alone.'

'More time for work,' I agreed.

'No, because you can never make up your mind about anything,' he said.

'But only with things that aren't important,' I protested.

'Nothing's important to you then,' he said disgustedly.

'Ted, if you want me to go, I'll go.'

And suddenly he shouted, 'God, how did we ever get married? Do you ever make any decisions for yourself? What would you have done with your life if I hadn't married you?'

I was terribly shocked at the time. But now I realize he knew what he was saying. Because later that evening he phoned from Los Angeles and said he wanted a divorce.

When something that violent hits you, you can't help losing your balance and falling. And after picking yourself up, you realize you can't trust anybody to save you – not your husband, not your mother, not God. So what can you do to stop yourself falling again?

My mother believed in God for many years. She said it was faith that kept all these good things coming our way, only I thought she said 'fate', because she couldn't say the 'th' sound in 'faith' properly. And later, I discovered that maybe it was fate all along, that faith was just a feeling that somehow you're in control.

The day I started thinking this was the day my mother lost her faith in God. We had gone to the beach for the first time as a family, because my father wanted to do some fishing. Although he knew nothing about fishing, he believed in his *nengkan*, his ability to do anything he really wanted. It was this belief in their *nengkan* that had brought my parents to America. It had enabled them to have seven children and buy a house, with very little money. It had given them the confidence to believe God was on their side, their ancestors were pleased with them, and that all the elements were in place, the right amount of wind and water.

So there we were on the beach, my father fishing off a rock, my mother unpacking some food, my older sisters running through the shallow waves, and me looking after my four young brothers. I was annoyed that I couldn't play with my sisters, because it was my duty to keep an eye on the boys. Matthew, Mark and Luke were all old enough to play sensibly on the sand, but the youngest, Bing, was only four and easily bored. I watched him carefully, calling out every now and then, 'Don't go too close to the water, Bing.' I sounded like my mother, constantly worried about her children's safety.

My mother believed that children were in greater danger on certain days, depending on their Chinese date of birth. This was explained in a book called *The Twenty-Six Malignant Gates*, which showed pictures of the terrible dangers that waited for young innocent children. And even though the birth dates meant only one danger per child, my mother worried about them all.

Bing begins to walk out along the rock where my father is.

'I'm going to see Daddy,' he says.

I see him calling to my father, who looks round towards him. How glad I am that my father is going to watch Bing for a while!

I hear shouts behind me. Luke and Mark are fighting. I turn to pull Luke off Mark, and in the confusion of the fight, nobody notices Bing except me. I look up and see him walk to the edge of the rock. And I think, *He's going to fall in.* Then there is a splash, and he disappears.

I sank to my knees, not speaking. I couldn't make sense of it. Then one of my sisters said, 'Where's Bing?' And suddenly there was shouting and sand flying as we rushed to the water's edge.

We were there for many hours, until sunset, when the search boats put their lights on. And later, when the police said it was time to give up, my mother went for a swim. She had never swum in her life, but her faith in her own *nengkan* convinced her she could do what these Americans couldn't. She could find Bing.

And when the rescue people pulled her out of the sea, her hair and clothes all heavy with the cold water, she remained calm. And although the police thought nothing more could be done, and sent us home, my mother was not ready to give up.

She woke me the next morning when it was still dark. 'Come with me,' she whispered. I assumed this was my punishment, as I hadn't watched Bing carefully enough, and that is why he had died. She and I got into the family car, and I was amazed to see her start the engine. All the way to the beach, I wondered how she had learned to drive overnight.

When we arrived, we walked to the rock where Bing had disappeared. In her hand she held the Bible, and looking out over the dark water, she called to God in her small voice. 'I have

My mother saw Bing three times, waving to her from the sea.

always believed in you,' she cried. 'We have always tried to show you our deepest respect. We went to your house. We brought you money. We sang your songs. You gave us our children. And now we have misplaced one of them. We were careless, this is true. So maybe you hid him from us to teach us a lesson. I have learned the lesson. And now I am here to take Bing back.'

I listened, horrified, to my mother's prayer. And I began to cry when she added, 'Forgive us for his bad manners. My daughter, this one here, will be sure to teach him better lessons of obedience before he visits you again.'

So great was her faith that she saw Bing three times, waving to her from the sea. But the third time he became just a piece of floating wood carried high on a wave.

My mother's back was still straight and her chin high, as she put the Bible down on the beach, and turned to me. 'An ancestor of ours once stole water from a secret place. Now the water is trying to steal back. We must give the spirit who lives in the sea another precious thing. Then he will give Bing back.'

She opened her hand to show me the valuable ring with a blue stone that her mother had given her, many years before. She threw the ring into the water. Suddenly she pointed and said, 'There!' And I too saw Bing walking at the far end of the beach. The hunger in our hearts was instantly filled. And then we saw him light a cigarette, grow tall, and become a stranger.

At that moment and not until that moment did she give up. She had a look on her face that I'll never forget. It was one of complete despair and horror, for losing Bing, for being so foolish as to think she could use faith to change fate.

I know now that I had never expected to find Bing, just as I know that I will never find a way to save my marriage. But my mother insists, 'You must try. This is your fate, what you must do.'

'So what can I do?'

'You must think for yourself, what you must do. If someone tells you what to do, then you are not trying.'

I think about Bing, how I knew he was in danger, how I let it happen. I think about my marriage, how I had seen the signs, really I had. But I just let it happen. And I think now that fate is shaped half by expectation, half by inattention. But somehow, when you lose something, faith takes over. You have to pay attention to what you lost.

My mother still pays attention to what she lost. When she and I came home from the beach that day, she wrote three words on an empty page in the Bible: the word 'Deaths', with 'Bing Hsu' underneath it. Then she pushed the Bible under the kitchen table leg. It's always there to remind her.

When I was little, I used to believe everything my mother said, even when I didn't know what she meant. The power of her words was that strong. She said that if I listened to her, I would discover where true words came from. And if I didn't listen to her, she said my ear would bend too easily to other people, all saying words that had no lasting meaning, because they only expressed their own desires.

More than thirty years later, my mother was still trying to make me listen. A month after I told her that Ted and I were getting a divorce, I met her at church, at a neighbour's funeral.

'That one, we bought it,' she whispered, pointing to a large arrangement of red and yellow flowers. 'Thirty-four dollars. All artificial, so it will last for ever. You can pay me your share later. You have money?'

'Yes. Ted sent me a check.'

I stood up to sing with everyone else in the church, but my mother was staring at me. 'Why does he send you a check?'

I refused to answer, and kept on singing. So she answered her own question, tight-lipped. 'Because he's doing monkey business with someone else, that's why.'

Monkey business? Ted? I wanted to laugh – her choice of words, but also the idea! Cool, silent, hairless Ted, whose breathing didn't alter one bit in the height of passion?

'No, I don't think so,' I said. 'And I don't think we should talk about Ted.'

'You *should* talk about this with mother, because mother knows what is inside you. Otherwise you become confused.'

When I got home, I realized she was right. I *was* becoming confused. I had been talking to too many people about Ted leaving me, describing a different feeling to each one of them. So now I wasn't sure whether I was miserable, or angry, whether I wanted Ted back, or revenge on him.

And then I received a letter from Ted. It was a hurriedly written note attached to our divorce papers, along with another check, this time for ten thousand dollars. The note said: 'Sign in these four places. Here's a check to cover your bills until things are finalized.' And instead of being grateful, I felt hurt. Why had he sent the check with the documents? And why had he chosen to sign it with the pen I gave him for Christmas last year?

I sat there, trying to listen to my heart, to make the right decision. My mother once told me why I was so confused all the time. She said I was born without wood, so that I listened to too many people. 'A girl is like a young tree,' she said. 'You must stand tall and listen to your mother standing next to you. That is the only way to grow strong and straight. But if you bend to listen to other people, you will grow thin and weak, and you will fall to the ground with the first strong wind.'

But by the time she told me this, it was too late. I had already begun to bend. Over the years, I tried to choose between Chinese and American opinions. At first I thought the American ones were better. But it was only later that I discovered they gave me too many choices, so it was easy to get confused and pick the wrong thing.

That's how I felt about my situation with Ted. Perhaps he wanted to trick me into giving up, by persuading me to accept this check. Or perhaps he had sent me ten thousand dollars because he wanted to show he truly loved me.

I was about to put an end to all this by signing the papers, when suddenly I remembered the house. I thought to myself, I love this house. The big wooden door into the hall, the sunlight in the kitchen, the view of the city from the sitting room, the beautiful garden where Ted had planted so many flowers. I looked out of the window and saw the grass had turned brown, the flowers were dying, and the path was hardly visible any more. The garden had grown wild from months of being ignored.

Fifteen years of living in Ted's shadow meant that I was unable to make the simplest decisions. So for the next three days, I stayed in bed, getting up only to go to the bathroom or heat up some chicken soup. I stopped thinking, and slept.

On the fourth day, the phone rang. It was Ted. He said crossly that he'd been trying to ring me for the last three days, and reminded me I hadn't returned the documents to him yet. Then he said what he really wanted, which was worse than anything I could have imagined. He wanted the papers signed and returned, and he wanted the house, because he was planning to get married again, to another woman.

Before I could stop myself, I gasped. 'So you *were* doing monkey business with someone else?' And then for the first time in months, all the questions were gone. There were no choices. At last I felt free. And suddenly I started laughing.

'What's so funny?' said Ted angrily.

'Sorry,' I said, trying to control myself. His silence made me laugh even harder. 'Listen, Ted,' I gasped eventually, 'the best thing is for you to come over here after work tonight.'

'There's nothing to talk about, Rose.'

'I know. I just want to show you something. And don't worry, you'll get your papers.'

I had no plan. I knew only that I wanted Ted to see me one more time before the divorce.

What I showed him in the end was the garden. 'What a mess,' he said, as he looked sadly at the wilderness.

'I like it this way,' I said, walking through the long grass to stroke the heads of the overgrown vegetables.

'Where are the papers?' asked Ted finally.

I handed them to him and he took them without looking at them. 'You don't have to move out immediately,' he said. 'You'll need at least a month to find a place to live.'

'I've already found a place,' I said quickly, because right then I knew where I was going to live. 'Here.'

'What do you mean?' He frowned threateningly at me, an expression of his that used to terrify me.

Now I felt nothing, no fear, no anger. 'I'm staying. My lawyer will be sending you the documents.'

Ted looked down at the divorce papers and saw that I hadn't signed them. 'What exactly do you think you're doing?'

And the answer, the one that was important above everything else, ran through my body and fell from my lips: 'You can't just pull me out of your life and throw me away.'

I saw what I wanted: his eyes, confused, then frightened. The power of my words was that strong.

JING-MEI WOO

Daughter of Suyuan Woo

Best Quality

My mother believed you could be anything you wanted to be in America. This country was where all her hopes lay. She had come here in 1949 after losing everything in China: her parents, her family home, her first husband, and her two baby daughters. But she never looked back with regret. There were so many ways for things to get better. You could open a restaurant. You could buy a house with almost no cash. You could become rich. You could become instantly famous.

'Of course you can be prodigy, too,' she told me when I was nine. 'You can be best at anything. What does Auntie Lindo know? Her daughter, she is only best at tricks.'

We didn't immediately pick the right kind of prodigy. At first my mother thought I could be a second Shirley Temple, the child actress who had been a huge star in America. We watched her old movies on television as though they were training films. 'You watch,' my mother used to say. 'You can be like her!'

She took me to have a new haircut, which I liked. It made me look forward to becoming famous. In fact, I was just as excited as my mother. I imagined this prodigy part of me in many different ways – I was a singer, a dancer, a religious leader, a queen, a beauty. I was filled with a sense that I would soon become *perfect*. My parents would love me. I would never do anything wrong. I would never be criticized, or need to show anger.

But sometimes the prodigy in me became impatient. 'If you

don't hurry up and get me out of here, I'm disappearing for ever,' it warned. 'And then you'll always be nothing.'

My mother soon gave up the Shirley Temple idea, because she thought she could find something better. Every night after dinner, she would present me with new tests, taking her examples from stories of amazing children she had read about in magazines. She got these magazines from people whose houses she cleaned. There were children who knew the capital cities of all the American states and most European countries, children who could calculate numbers in their heads, say what the daily temperatures would be in Los Angeles, New York and London, look at a page of the Bible and then repeat every word, or stand on their heads without using their hands.

But I could do none of these things, and after seeing my mother's disappointed face again and again, something inside me began to die. I hated the tests, the raised hopes and failed expectations. Before going to bed one night, I looked in the mirror, and when I saw only my ordinary face there, I began to cry. And then I saw what seemed to be the prodigy side of me, staring back at me – an angry, powerful girl. She and I were the same. I began to have new thoughts. I won't let my mother change me, I promised myself. I won't be what I'm not.

So now when my mother presented her tests, I pretended to be bored. And I was. I performed so badly that I thought my mother was beginning to give up hope.

Two or three months went by without any mention of my being a prodigy again. And then one day my mother was watching television when I suddenly realized how hard she was concentrating on the program. 'Look!' she said urgently to me.

I could see why she was fascinated by it. A little Chinese girl, about nine years old, with a short straight haircut like mine, was playing the piano. She had the smiling confidence of Shirley

Temple, but she was proudly modest like a proper Chinese child.

'She play music note right, but doesn't sound good! No singing sound,' complained my mother.

'Why are you so hard on her?' I said carelessly. 'Maybe she's not the best, but she's trying hard.' I knew almost at once I would be sorry I had said that.

'Just like you. Not the best. Because you not trying.'

In spite of these warning signs, I wasn't worried. Our family had no piano, and couldn't afford to buy one, or pay for lessons.

Three days afterwards, my mother announced my timetable for piano lessons and practice. She had talked to Mr Chong, who lived on the first floor of our block. He was a retired piano teacher, and he had agreed to give me lessons and let me use his piano to practice on, between four and six o'clock every day. In exchange, my mother would clean his apartment.

When my mother told me this, I was furious. 'Why don't you like me the way I am?' I shouted. 'I'm not a musical prodigy!'

My mother smacked me. 'Who ask you be prodigy?' she shouted back. 'Only ask you be your best. For your sake! You think I want you be prodigy? Hnnh! What for? Who ask you?'

I soon found out why Mr Chong, whom I secretly called Old Chong, had retired from teaching. He was deaf. 'Like Beethoven!' he shouted to me. 'We're both listening only in our head!'

He taught me how to stretch my fingers, how to find the notes on the piano, and how to keep playing in time. As I played, he conducted in a dream-like way, smiling and clapping when I finished. When I ran my hands quickly over the black and white keys, playing some nonsense that sounded as if a cat had knocked over a pile of tin cans, he still smiled and clapped. And that's how I discovered Old Chong's eyes were too slow to keep up with the wrong notes I was playing.

This knowledge made me lazy, and I learnt to get away with mistakes. I never stopped to correct myself, but just kept on playing in time. And Old Chong kept conducting, as if in a dream. Maybe I never gave myself a fair chance. Maybe I might have become a good pianist at that young age. But I was so determined not to try, not to become anybody different from me.

Over the next year, I learnt and practiced like this. And then one day, after church, I heard my mother and her friend Lindo Jong boasting to each other about their daughters. Auntie Lindo's daughter, Waverly, was standing near me at the time. We had grown up together, sharing all the closeness of two sisters, quarreling over toys and sweets. In other words, for the most part, we hated each other. I thought she was too self-important. Waverly Jong was famous as Chinatown's chess prodigy.

'She bring home too many prizes,' complained Auntie Lindo. 'All day I do nothing but dust her winnings.' She threw a scolding look at Waverly, who pretended not to notice. 'You lucky you don't have this problem,' she said to my mother.

'Our problem worse than yours,' replied my mother. 'If we ask Jing-mei to wash dishes, she hear nothing but music. It's like you can't stop this natural talent.'

And right then I decided to put a stop to her foolish pride.

A few weeks later, Old Chong and my mother arranged for me to play in a talent show in the church hall. By then my parents had saved up enough to buy me a second-hand piano, which was the showpiece of our living room. For the competition, I was going to play a simple, moody piece that sounded more difficult than it was. While I was practicing this piece, I never really listened to what I was playing. At the time I was dreaming about being somewhere else, about being someone else.

My parents had invited all the families from the Joy Luck Club to witness my first public appearance as a musical prodigy. At first, when I stepped up to the piano in front of the audience, I was confident. It was as if I knew, without a doubt, that the prodigy side of me really did exist. And when I started to play, I was so caught up in how lovely I looked that I didn't worry how I would sound. So it was a surprise to me when I hit the first wrong note, and then another, and another. I played these strange, sour notes all the way to the end.

When I stood up, I discovered my legs were shaking. Maybe the audience, like Old Chong, had not heard anything wrong at all. I bowed low, looked up and smiled expectantly. The room was quiet, except for Old Chong, who was smiling and shouting, 'Well done!' The audience clapped weakly, and as I walked back to my chair, I tried hard not to cry. I heard a little boy whisper to his mother, 'That was awful,' and the mother whispered back, 'Well, she certainly tried.' Now I realized how many people were in the audience, the whole world, it seemed. I was aware of eyes burning into my back. I felt the shame of my mother and father as they sat stiffly, with fixed smiles, through the rest of the show.

At the end of the competition, the Joy Luck Club families came up to my parents.

'Lots of talented children,' Auntie Lindo said casually.

Waverly looked at me and smiled. 'You aren't a prodigy like me,' she said confidently, shaking her head.

But the worst thing was my mother's expression: a quiet, vacant look that said she had lost everything. And when we got home, she walked straight through into the back bedroom and closed the door. No accusations. No blame. In a way, I felt disappointed. I had been waiting for her to start shouting, so I could shout back and cry and blame her for all my misery.

I assumed that my talent-show failure meant I would never have to play the piano again. But two days later, my mother reminded me it was four o'clock and time to do some practice.

'I'm not going to play any more,' I replied. 'Why should I? I'm not musical.' I saw how angry that made her. She pulled me off the sofa and dragged me towards the piano. 'No!' I screamed, resisting with all my strength. 'You want me to be someone I'm not! I'll never be the kind of daughter you want me to be!'

'Only two kinds of daughters,' she shouted back. 'Those who are obedient and those who follow their own mind! Only one kind of daughter can live in this house. Obedient daughter!'

'Then I wish I wasn't your daughter!' I shouted.

'Too late change this,' screamed my mother.

I wanted to see her anger spill over. And that's when I

I bowed low, and the audience clapped weakly.

remembered the babies she had lost in China, the ones we never talked about. 'Then I wish I'd never been born!' I shouted. 'I wish I were dead! Like *them*.'

It was as if I had said a magic word. Her face went still, her mouth closed, her arms dropped to her sides, and she walked backwards out of the room, as if she were blowing away, like a small brown leaf, thin and lifeless.

It was not the only disappointment my mother felt in me. In the years that followed, I failed her so many times. Because, unlike her, I did not believe I could be anything I wanted to be. I could only be me.

And for all those years, we never talked about my piano-playing or the talent show or the terrible things I had said to her. So I never found a way to ask her why she had hoped for something so large that failure was bound to come. And even worse, I never asked her the question that frightened me the most: Why had she given up hope?

But a few years ago, she offered to give me the piano for my thirtieth birthday. I had not played in all those years. I saw the offer as a sign of forgiveness.

'Are you sure?' I asked shyly. 'Won't you and Dad miss it?'

'No, this your piano,' she said firmly. 'Always your piano. You only one can play.'

'Well, I probably can't play any more,' I said.

'You have natural talent,' said my mother. 'You could been prodigy if you wanted. You just not trying.' She seemed neither angry nor sad, as if she were simply stating a fact.

In the end I left the piano at my parents' flat. It wasn't until after my mother's death that I tried playing it again, and then I was surprised to discover how easily it came back to me.

Five months ago, my mother invited her long-time friends Lindo and Tin Jong, their son Vincent, and their daughter Waverly to dinner to celebrate the Chinese New Year. Vincent was bringing his girlfriend, Lisa Lum, and Waverly was coming with Rich Schields, the man she was going to marry, as well as her four-year-old daughter Shoshana. We also invited Mr Chong, my old piano teacher. With my parents and me, that made eleven people. But my mother only counted ten, because to her way of thinking, Shoshana was just a child and didn't count. She hadn't considered that Waverly might not think the same way.

I finished work early to help my mother do the shopping. Together we wandered from one fish shop to another to find the most energetic crabs. 'Don't get a dead one,' warned my mother. 'Even a beggar won't eat a dead one.' Eventually we found ten healthy ones. Then my mother added an eleventh, as an extra one, although it had a missing leg, which she said was unlucky.

When our guests were all sitting down, the dish of steaming hot crabs was passed around. Waverly was first, and she picked the best one and put it on her daughter's plate. Then she picked the next best for Rich and another good one for herself. And because she had learnt the skill of choosing the best from her mother, it was only natural that Auntie Lindo knew how to pick the next best ones for her husband, her son, his girlfriend, and herself. And my mother, of course, gave the one that looked the best to Old Chong, because he was nearly ninety and deserved that kind of respect, and then picked another good one for my father. That left two on the plate for me to choose from: a large one and number eleven with the missing leg.

I'm not too fond of crab, because I know it's boiled alive, but I knew I couldn't refuse. I thought I was doing the right thing, taking the crab with the missing leg. But my mother cried, 'No! You eat big one. I cannot finish.'

I remember the hungry eating sounds everybody else was making, and my mother's quiet plate. I was the only one who saw her take her untouched crab out to the kitchen and return with an empty plate. And then, as our stomachs filled, everybody started talking at once.

Uncle Tin told a joke he must have practiced many times. 'I tell my daughter, Hey, why be poor? Marry rich!' He laughed loudly, then explained to Lisa Lum, who was sitting next to him, 'Hey, don't you get it? What happen? She's going to marry him. Because I tell her to – *marry Rich*.'

Waverly said to me, 'You should try my hairdresser. He's great, though he probably charges more than you're used to.'

I felt like screaming. I wanted to embarrass her in front of everybody. So I decided to remind her about the work I'd done for her company lately, eight pages of advertising material I'd written and still hadn't received payment for. 'Maybe I could afford his prices,' I said, 'if your company paid me on time.'

I was pleased to see she was speechless for a moment. But then she sighed and said, 'Listen, June, I don't know how to tell you this, but – well, we decided your work was unacceptable.'

'You're lying. You said it was fine.'

She sighed again. 'I just didn't want to hurt your feelings.'

I felt I was drowning in deep water. 'It's . . . normal not to be perfect first time. I can rewrite it. Just tell me which parts—'

'Sorry, June. The style's just not right for us. I'm sure your other customers are happy with your material, but we're a big company. Really, we need a bit more than you can provide.'

And then I heard my mother say, 'True, cannot teach style. Must be born this way. June not smart like you.'

Waverly had beaten me again, and my own mother had betrayed me. That was the night I realized I was good at what I did in my own small world, but would not succeed if I aimed any higher. Suddenly I no longer felt angry at Waverly, but tired and foolish, as if I'd been running to escape from someone chasing me, only to look behind and discover no one there.

After everybody had left, my mother and I washed the dishes in the kitchen.

'What happened to your crab, Ma?' I asked.

'Not so good. That crab die. Even a beggar don't want.'

'How could you tell? I didn't smell anything wrong.'

'Can tell even before cook! Crab already dying.'

'What if someone else had chosen that crab?'

My mother smiled. 'Only *you* choose that crab. Nobody else take it. Everybody else want best quality. You thinking different.' Then she took off the gold chain that she always wore, with the piece of jade hanging from it, and put it in my hand.

'No, Ma,' I protested. 'I can't take this.'

'Take it, take it. For a long time, I wanted to give you this. See, I wore it on my skin, so when you put it on your skin, then you know my meaning. This is your life's importance.'

I looked unhappily at the necklace. 'You're giving me this only because of what Waverly said tonight.'

'Tss! Why you listen to her? She is like a crab. Always walking sideways, never forwards. You can go another way.'

I put the necklace on. It felt cool on my skin. But it wasn't the kind of jewellery I would have chosen for myself, so when I got home, I put it away in a box.

But these days I wear it every day, and think about my life's importance. I wonder what it means, because my mother died three months ago, just before my thirty-sixth birthday. And she's the only person I could have asked, to tell me about life's importance, to help me understand my sorrow.

Queen Mother
of the Western Skies

'O! You bad little thing!' said the woman, smiling
at her baby granddaughter. 'Are you laughing for
no reason?' As the baby continued to laugh, the
woman felt a deep wish rising in her heart.

'Even if I could live for ever,' she said to the
baby, 'I still don't know which way I would teach
you. I was once so free and innocent. I too laughed
for no reason.

'But later I threw away my foolish innocence to
protect myself. And then I taught my daughter,
your mother, to throw away her innocence so she
would not be hurt either.

'Was this kind of thinking wrong? If I now
recognize evil in other people, is it not because I
have become evil too?'

The baby laughed, listening to her grandmother's sad words.

'O! O! You say you are laughing because you
have already lived for ever, over and over again?
You say you are Syi Wang Mu, Queen Mother of
the Western Skies, now come back to give me the
answer! Good, good, I am listening . . .

'Thank you, little Queen. Then you must teach
my daughter this same lesson. How to lose your
innocence but not your hope. How to laugh for
ever.'

AN-MEI HSU
Mother of Rose Hsu Jordan

Magpies

Yesterday my daughter said to me, 'My marriage is falling apart.'

And now all she can do is watch it falling. She sits on a sofa, pouring tears out about this shame. And I think she will sit there until there is nothing more to fall, nothing left to cry about.

She cried, 'No choice! No choice!' But she is choosing to do nothing. If she doesn't try, she can lose her chance for ever.

I know this, because I was brought up the Chinese way: I was taught to desire nothing, to swallow other people's misery, to eat my own bitterness. And even though I taught my daughter the opposite, still she came out the same way! Maybe it is because she was born to me and she was born a girl. And I was born to my mother and I was born a girl. All of us are like stairs, one step after another, all going the same way.

I know how it is to listen and watch, as if your life were a dream. You can close your eyes when you no longer want to watch. But when you no longer want to listen, what can you do? I can still hear what happened more than sixty years ago.

When my mother first arrived at my uncle's house in Ningpo, I was nine years old and could not remember ever seeing her. But I knew she was my mother, because I could feel her pain.

'Do not look at that woman,' my aunt warned me. 'She has thrown her face into the eastward-flowing stream. Her ancestral spirit is lost forever. The person you see is evil, rotten to the bone.'

And I stared at my mother, who did not look evil to me. It is true she wore strange foreign clothes. But she did not speak back when my aunt cursed her. And she cried from her heart when Popo died, even though Popo, her mother, had sent her away so many years before. Now she was preparing to return to the city of Tientsin, where she had dishonoured her widowhood by becoming the third concubine to a rich man.

How could she leave without me? This was a question I could not ask. I was a child. I could only watch and listen.

The night before she was to leave, she held my head against her body, as if to protect me from a danger I could not see. I was crying to bring her back before she was even gone.

'An-mei,' she whispered, 'have you seen the little turtle that lives in the pool in the courtyard?' I nodded. 'I also knew that turtle when I was a small child,' she continued. 'He is a very old turtle. This turtle feeds on our thoughts. I discovered this one day, when I was your age. Popo told me that I could no longer be a child, that I could not shout or run or play, but must be silent and sensible and obedient. After she had told me this, I sat by the pool, looking into the water. And because I was weak, I began to cry. Then I saw this turtle, swimming to the surface. He opened his mouth and swallowed my tears, five, six, seven of them, as soon as they touched the water. Then he climbed out of the pool, crawled on to a smooth rock, and began to speak.

'The turtle said, "I have eaten your tears, and this is why I know your misery. But I must warn you. If you cry, your life will always be sad."

'Then he opened his mouth, and out poured five, six, seven beautiful eggs. The eggs broke open and seven birds came out. They immediately began to sing. I knew from their snow-white stomachs and pretty voices that they were magpies, birds of joy. When I reached out my hand to catch one, they all rose up, beat their black wings in my face, and flew up into the air, laughing.

'"Now you see," said the turtle, diving back into the pool, "why it is useless to cry. Your tears do not wash away your sorrows. They feed someone else's joy. And that is why you must learn to swallow your own tears."'

But after my mother finished her story, I looked at her and saw she was crying. And I also began to cry again, thinking that this was our fate, to live like two turtles seeing the watery world together from the bottom of the little pool.

In the morning I woke up to hear, not the bird of joy, but angry shouting from the courtyard beneath my window. There I could see my mother on her knees, her back rounded like the turtle in the pool, in front of my uncle. 'You want to take your daughter and destroy her life as well!' he was shouting. My mother said nothing, but she was crying. I began to cry too, swallowing the bitter tears.

I got dressed and hurried downstairs. Forgetting my auntie's commands, I shouted, 'Ma!'

My mother stood up and held out her hand to me. 'An-mei, I am not asking you to come. But I am going back to Tientsin now and you can follow me.'

Now my uncle picked up a vase. 'Is this what you want to do?' he asked me. 'Throw your life away? If you follow this woman, you can never lift your head again.' He threw the vase on the ground, where it smashed into many pieces.

My mother took my hand. 'Come, An-mei,' she said.

As I walked away from my uncle's dark house, I wondered if what he had said was true. So I tried to lift my head. And I saw my little brother, crying so hard as my auntie held onto his hand. My mother did not dare to take him too. A son can never go to somebody else's house to live. But I knew he was angry and afraid, because my mother had not asked him to follow. What my uncle had said was true. After I saw my brother this way, I could not keep my head lifted.

We traveled for seven days, one day by train, six days by ship. At first, my mother was very cheerful. She told me stories of Tientsin to take my mind off the past. She described the delicious food you could buy from street-sellers, the fresh fish that arrived every day at the port, the foreigners who lived in houses of strange shapes and colors, and the snow that covered the city in wintertime. Her words made me look forward to my new home.

But on the fifth day, I became fearful. At night I dreamed of the eastward-flowing stream that my aunt had spoken about, the dark waters that changed a person for ever. And I saw how my mother was already beginning to change, how dark and angry her face had become, looking out over the sea, thinking her own thoughts. And my thoughts, too, became cloudy and confused.

On the day of our arrival in Tientsin, she took off her white Chinese widow's dress and put on a stylish European dress, with a matching brown hat. She painted her eyebrows black and her lips red. This was a shocking sight. She was no longer paying respect to my dead father, but was making her shame public.

But she had thought of me, too. She gave me a large box with a beautiful new white dress and shoes in it, and helped me to put the things on. When I was dressed, she looked at me and said,

'An-mei, now you are ready to start your new life. You will live in a new house. You will have a new father, Wu Tsing. Many sisters. Another little brother. Dresses and good things to eat. Do you think all this will be enough to make you happy?'

I nodded quietly, thinking about the unhappiness of my brother in Ningpo. My mother did not say anything more.

Wu Tsing was a very rich businessman, whose house was in the best part of the city. Everything about it spoke of his wealth and importance. It had been built in the Western style; Wu Tsing liked foreign things because foreigners had made him rich.

When we arrived, a young woman ran out and greeted my mother with cries of joy. She was Yan Chang, my mother's personal servant, and she showed me round the enormous house. There were so many rooms, and such beautiful furniture, and so many people! My uncle's house in Ningpo had been quite impressive, but this house in Tientsin was amazing. I thought to myself, my uncle was wrong. There was no shame in my mother's marrying Wu Tsing.

I was so happy those first few nights, in this fascinating house, sleeping in the big soft bed in my mother's room. My mother seemed to recover her pleasant nature. During the daytime we played games and talked and laughed together, and at night she told me stories as I lay in her arms falling asleep. But I remember clearly when all that comfort became no longer comfortable.

Two weeks after our arrival I was playing in the large garden, when I saw two shiny black rickshaws and a large motorcar arrive. Servants poured out of the rickshaws, and one held the car door open, as a young and pretty girl stepped out. She looked very proud, although she was only a few years older than me.

Then the servants reached into the back of the car, and I saw a man being lifted by both arms. This was Wu Tsing. He was much older than my mother, a short, fat man wearing Western clothes. As soon as his shoes touched the ground, he walked towards the house, ignoring everybody, even though people were greeting him and were busy opening doors and carrying his bags. The young girl followed him inside, smiling at everyone, as if they were there to honour her.

I looked up at the house and saw my mother looking down from her window. So in this clumsy way, my mother found out that Wu Tsing had taken his fourth concubine. Still, my mother was not jealous of this young girl, who would now be called Fifth Wife. Why should she be? My mother did not love Wu Tsing. A girl in China did not marry for love, but for position, and my mother's position, I later learnt, was the worst.

A few days after Wu Tsing arrived home, my mother woke me up in the middle of the night. 'An-mei, be a good girl,' she said in a tired voice. 'Go to Yan Chang's room now.' I saw a dark shadow and began to cry. It was Wu Tsing. 'Be quiet. Nothing is the matter. Go now,' my mother whispered. And when I went to Yan Chang, I knew she was expecting me to come.

The next morning I could not look at my mother. But I saw that Fifth Wife had been crying, and at breakfast she was rude to everybody. But later that morning she was smiling again, and showing off a new dress and new shoes.

In the afternoon, my mother spoke of her unhappiness for the first time. 'Do you see how shameful my life is?' she cried. 'He's brought home a new wife, a girl with no manners, from the muddy back streets! He bought her for a few dollars! And at night, when he can no longer use her, he comes to me, smelling of her mud.' She was crying now. 'An-mei, you can see now, a fourth wife is less than a fifth wife. I was a first wife once, your father's wife, a respected woman. Do not forget this, An-mei!'

When the cold weather came, Second Wife and Third Wife, their children and their servants all returned home to Tientsin. While the servants were unloading luggage from the rickshaws, Third Wife stepped out of the car first, a plain, sensible-looking woman with three daughters who looked very much like her. Then came Second Wife, wearing a long fur coat and very expensive Western clothes, carrying a little boy in her arms. We greeted these ladies politely. Second Wife walked towards me, examining me carefully. Then she smiled, took off her valuable-looking necklace and put it round my neck. My mother immediately protested that it was too precious a gift for a small child, but Second Wife insisted. I could see that my mother was angry, but I really wanted to keep the necklace.

Later, my mother said to me, 'Be careful, An-mei. She is trying to trick you, so you will do anything for her.'

I was trying not to listen to my mother. I was thinking how much she complained, and that perhaps all her unhappiness came from her complaints.

'Give the necklace to me,' she said suddenly. I did not move. 'I will not let her buy you for such a cheap price,' she said, and lifted the necklace over my head. And before I could stop her, she put the necklace under her shoe and stepped on it. I saw that it was broken. This necklace that had almost bought my heart and mind was only made of cheap glass.

'Now can you recognize what is true?' she asked. And I nodded. She put something in my hand. It was a heavy ring with a great watery blue stone in the centre, a blue so pure that I never stopped looking at that ring with wonder.

In the next month, First Wife returned from her house in Peking. I remember thinking that she would make Second Wife bow to her commands. First Wife was the head wife by law and by custom. But First Wife seemed to be a living ghost, no threat to Second Wife, whose spirit was very strong.

Yan Chang told me that Wu Tsing's and First Wife's marriage had been arranged by a matchmaker. But when First Wife had given birth to two girls who both had physical faults, she turned to religion for comfort, and spent most of her time praying and smoking opium in her room. Wu Tsing made a mid-morning visit to her room once a week, drinking tea for half an hour and inquiring about her health. He did not bother her at night.

This ghost of a woman should have caused no suffering to my mother, but in fact she put ideas into my mother's head. 'We too are going to have a house of our own,' she told me happily. 'It will be a small one, but we can live there by ourselves, with Yan Chang and a few other servants. Wu Tsing has promised.'

That winter I spent a lot of time with Yan Chang, who told me all about Second Wife. Apparently she had been a famous singer, popular with the male audiences in the teahouses. Wu Tsing had asked her to be his concubine, not for love, but in order to own what so many men desired. And after she had seen his enormous wealth and his weak-spirited first wife, she said yes.

From the start she knew how to control him. She knew that he was afraid of ghosts. So when he refused to let her have more money, she pretended to kill herself; she ate raw opium, enough to make her sick, and then sent her servant to tell Wu Tsing she was dying. He was frightened that her ghost would come to take revenge on him, and three days later she had even more money than she had asked for. She played this trick again and again, so that soon she had a better room in the house, her own private rickshaw, and a house for her elderly parents as well.

But one thing she could not have: children. So before Wu Tsing could complain about her inability to provide him with a son, she herself selected a new concubine for him. Third Wife was so plain that she had no chance of marrying otherwise, and she was very grateful to Second Wife for arranging this. For this reason Second Wife was able to keep her position as head wife.

Later on, when it seemed that Third Wife could only produce daughters, Second Wife chose my mother as third concubine and Fourth Wife. She set a trap for my mother, who, being only a worthless widow, had no way to escape. Three years later she gave birth to a son, whom Second Wife claimed as her own.

And that was how I learned that the baby Syaudi was really my mother's son, and my little half-brother.

After Yan Chang told me this story, I saw Second Wife's truly evil nature. I knew why my mother cried in her room so often. Wu Tsing's promise of a house, for becoming the mother of his only son, had disappeared the day Second Wife made another pretended attempt to kill herself. And my mother knew she could do nothing to bring the promise back.

Two days before the new year, Yan Chang woke me while it was still dark. 'Quickly!' she cried, and hurried me to my mother's room. It was brightly lit, and Wu Tsing, Second Wife, Third Wife, Fifth Wife and the doctor were all standing round the bed. My mother lay on the bed, her arms and legs marching like a soldier's, her tongue swollen, her face pale. She had taken poison. We could do nothing but stand silently at her bedside.

I remembered her story about the little turtle, his warning not to cry. And I wanted to tell her it was no use. There were already too many tears. And I tried to swallow them one by one, but I fainted and was carried back to Yan Chang's bed. So that morning, while my mother was dying, I was dreaming. I was falling into a pool, where I became a little turtle. Above me I could see a thousand magpies drinking from the pool, singing happily and filling their snow-white stomachs. I was crying hard, so many tears, but they drank and drank, until I had no more tears left and the pool was empty, everything as dry as sand.

My mother had planned her death so carefully that it became a weapon. The third day after someone dies, their spirit comes back to collect what is owing. For my mother, that day was the first of the new year, when all debts must be paid, or disaster and misfortune will follow.

So on that day, Wu Tsing, fearful of her ghost, made a promise to bring me and Syaudi up as his honoured children.

And on that day, I showed Second Wife the broken glass necklace and smashed the remains of it under my foot.

And on that day, Second Wife's hair began to turn white.

And on that day, I learnt to shout.

I know how it is to live your life like a dream. To listen and watch, to wake up and try to understand what has already happened. My mother, she suffered. She lost her face and tried to hide it. She found only greater misery and finally could not hide that. That was what people did in the past. They had no choice; it was their fate.

But these days they can do something else. They no longer have to swallow their own tears or put up with the cruel laughter of magpies. They say, 'Enough of this suffering and silence!' and they clap their hands and shout, to drive the magpies away.

The magpies drank and drank, until I had no more tears left.

Waiting Between the Trees

My daughter has put me in the tiniest of rooms in her new house. 'This is the guest bedroom,' Lena said in her proud American way. I smiled. But to Chinese ways of thinking, the guest bedroom is the best bedroom, which she and her husband use.

I do not tell her this, even though I love my daughter, because she does not want to learn wisdom from me. When she was born, she jumped away from me like a slippery fish, and has been swimming away ever since. All her life, I have watched her as though from another shore. And now I must tell her everything about my past. It is the only way to get under her skin, and pull her to where she can be saved.

This room is like a box for a dead person's body. I should remind my daughter not to put any babies in this room. But she has already said she doesn't want any babies. She and her husband are too busy drawing places that someone else will build and someone else will eat in or live in.

What good does it do to draw beautiful buildings and <u>then</u> live in one that is useless? Everything in this house is for looking at, not for using. Like this table, on its thin legs. A person must remember not to put a heavy bag on this table, or it will break, and then the vase with the flower in it will fall and break too.

All around this house I see the signs. My daughter looks but does not see. This is a house that will break into pieces. How do I know? I have always known a thing before it happens.

When I was a young girl, I was wild and selfish. I was small and pretty, too proud to listen to my mother, who loved me too much to scold me. We were one of the richest families in our town, so I could wear whatever clothes I wanted and have as many servants as I liked.

I remember the night my youngest aunt got married. I was sixteen. The ceremony was over, but many of my relations were still sitting round the big table in the main room, laughing and eating fruit and roasted seeds. A friend of my aunt's new husband was sitting with us, his face reddened from drinking whiskey.

'Ying-ying,' he called to me, 'are you still hungry?' I nodded at him, hoping for some cake. But instead he pulled out a large water melon and put it on the table. 'Open the water melon!' he said, pushing a sharp knife into the perfect fruit. As he laughed, his huge mouth opened so wide that I could see all the way back to his gold teeth. Everybody laughed loudly, and my face burned with embarrassment, because I did not understand.

I was innocent then. I did not know what an evil thing he did when he cut open that water melon. I did not understand until six months later when I was married to him and he whispered drunkenly to me that he was ready to 'open the water melon'.

This was a man so bad that even today I cannot speak his name. Why did I marry him? It was because, the day after my aunt's wedding, I began to know a thing before it happened.

My half-sisters and I were sitting drinking tea and eating roasted water melon seeds. They were talking about the boys they hoped to marry.

When they asked me, I answered proudly, 'I know of no one,' because I considered none of the boys good enough for me. But then, maybe because of the water melon seeds I was eating, I thought of that laughing man from the night before.

And just then, a wind blew in from the north and a flower on the table fell at my feet. It was as if a knife had cut the flower's head off as a sign. Right then, I knew I would marry this man.

And soon we were engaged, and then married. My daughter does not know that I was married to this man, twenty years before she was even born. She does not know how beautiful I was then, or, strange to say, how much I loved him.

The night he planted the baby, I again knew a thing before it happened. I knew it was a boy; I could see him inside me. It's because I had such joy then that I came to have so much hate.

My husband began to take many business trips to the north. I remembered the north wind had blown luck and my husband my way, so at night, when he was away, I opened wide my bedroom window to blow his spirit and heart back to me. What I did not know is that the north wind is the coldest. It takes all warmth away. It was so strong that it blew my husband past my bedroom and out of the back door. I found out he had gone to live with a singer, and there were many others he had slept with.

So I will tell Lena of my shame, that I was abandoned by my husband when I was only eighteen, that I lost my prettiness, that I thought of killing myself, that I killed my baby before it was born, because I came to hate this man so much.

When my daughter looks at me, she sees a small old lady. That is because she has no *chuming*, no way of knowing things inside. If she had *chuming*, she would see a tiger lady, because I was born in the year of the Tiger. A tiger has two sides, gold and black. The gold side attacks, with a fierce heart. The black side is clever, and stands still, hiding its gold between the trees, seeing and not being seen, waiting patiently for things to come. I did not learn to use my black side until after the bad man had left me.

For ten years I lived in the country with a cousin's family. If you ask me what I did during these long years, I can only say I waited between the trees. Then I moved to the city and started work selling clothes in a large shop. It was here that I met Clifford St Clair. I knew that I would marry him. I neither liked nor disliked him, but I knew he was the sign that the black side of me would soon go away. But I did not agree to marry him until, in 1946, I received a letter from my aunt telling me my husband was dead.

St Clair took me to America, where I learnt Western ways and gave birth to a daughter, also a Tiger. Can I tell her that I loved her father? I knew he loved me with all his heart. How could I not love him? But it was the love of a ghost. Arms that encircled but did not touch. A bowl full of rice, but with no hunger to eat it.

Now St Clair is dead. He and I can now love equally. He knows the things I have been hiding all these years. Now I must tell my daughter everything, that she is the daughter of a ghost. This is my greatest shame. How can I leave this world without leaving her my spirit? So I will gather together my past. The pain that cut my spirit loose, I will hold in my hand until it becomes hard and shiny. And then my fierceness can come back, my golden side. I will use this sharp pain to get under my daughter's tough skin and cut her tiger spirit loose.

I know a thing before it happens. She will hear the vase and table crashing to the floor. She will come up to my room. Her eyes will see nothing in the darkness, where I am waiting between the trees.

Double Face

My daughter wanted to go to China for her wedding trip, but now she is afraid. 'What if they think I'm one of them?' she asked me. 'What if they don't let me come back to the United States?'

'When you go to China,' I told her, 'you don't even need to open your mouth. They already know you're an outsider.'

'What are you talking about?' she asked. My daughter likes to speak back, and question what I say.

'Aii-ya,' I said. 'They know, just watching the way you walk, the way you carry your face. They know you do not belong.'

My daughter did not look pleased when I told her that she didn't look Chinese. Maybe ten years ago, she would have thought it was good news. But now she wants to be Chinese, because it's so fashionable. And I know it's too late. All those years I tried to teach her! She followed my Chinese ways only until she learnt how to walk out of the door by herself and go to school. Only her skin and hair are Chinese; inside, she is all American-made. She cannot even speak Chinese.

It's my fault she is this way. I wanted my children to have American circumstances and Chinese character. How could I know these two things do not mix? I taught her how American circumstances work. If you are born poor here, it's no lasting shame; the government gives you money. If the roof crashes down on your head, no need to cry over this bad luck; the lawyers will make the owner repair it. In America, nobody says you have to keep the circumstances you find yourself in.

She learnt these things, but I couldn't teach her about Chinese character. How to obey parents and listen to your mother's mind. How not to show your own thoughts, how to know your own worth. Why Chinese thinking is best. She never learnt this.

My daughter is getting married a second time. So she's asked me to go to her hairdresser, Mr Rory. I know her meaning. She is ashamed of my looks. What will her husband's parents and his important lawyer friends think of this old-fashioned, elderly Chinese woman? I sit in the chair in front of the mirror at Mr Rory's, while he and my daughter discuss me and my hair. Do they think I don't understand English? She is my daughter and I am proud of her, and I am her mother but she is not proud of me.

Mr Rory looks at both of us. Then he says something that really displeases her. 'It's amazing how much you two look alike!'

I smile, but Waverly's eyes become very narrow, like a cat's. Mr Rory goes away, and Waverly and I are left looking at each other's faces in the mirror. She is frowning.

'You can see your character in your face,' I say to her without thinking. 'You can see your future.'

'What do you mean?' she says.

And now I have to fight back my feelings. These two faces are so much the same! The same happiness, the same sadness, the same good fortune, the same faults. Like the faces of myself and my mother, back in China, when I was a young girl.

My mother, your grandmother, once told me my fortune. She was sitting in front of a big mirror in her bedroom, while I looked over her shoulder. 'You are lucky,' she said to me. 'Your ears are the right shape, but you must listen to your opportunities. You have my nose, straight and smooth; that's a good sign. A girl with a crooked nose is bound to have misfortune. Your chin is not too long and not too short, so you will have a long life, but not too long. Your eyes are eager yet respectful; you will be a good wife and mother. And your hair grows low on your forehead, which means you will have some hardships in your early life. But look at my hairline now! It's high – such a good thing for my old age. Later you will learn to worry and lose your hair too.'

When my mother told me these things, I was only ten. I wanted to look and be just like her. This was before our circumstances separated us: a flood that caused my family to leave me behind, my first marriage to a family who did not want me, a terrible war, and later, an ocean that took me to a new country. My mother never saw how my face changed over the years, how I began to worry but still did not lose my hair, how my nose became crooked when I fell on a crowded bus in San Francisco, how my eyes began to follow the American way.

It's hard to keep your Chinese face in America. Before I even arrived there, I had to hide my true self. In Peking I found a Chinese girl who had been brought up in America, and I paid her to tell me how to behave, what to say and what to do.

'You cannot say you want to live there for ever,' this girl told me. 'You must say you want to study there, and then return to China to teach Chinese people what you have learnt.'

'What should I say I want to learn?' I asked.

'Religion,' she replied. 'Then they will respect you. Then when you are allowed in, you must find a husband. An American citizen is best.' She saw my look of surprise, and quickly added, 'He must be Chinese-born, of course. But if he does not have permission to stay, you must immediately have a baby. Once it has arrived, it is an American citizen and can do anything it wants. It can ask its mother to stay. You understand?'

In fact, when I arrived in America, nobody asked me any questions at all. I rented an apartment at an address in San Francisco given to me by this girl, and started work in a factory making cookies. It was exhausting work, but by the end of the first week I had got used to it, and was able to talk to the woman next to me. This is how I met An-mei Hsu, your Auntie An-mei. She showed me how each little cake had to be wrapped in a piece of paper, with writing on it. She read out some of them to me, and explained them in Chinese. 'You can't teach an old dog new tricks.' 'Accept defeat and live to fight another day.' 'One man's meat is another man's poison.'

'But what is this nonsense?' I asked, puzzled.

'They are fortunes,' she said. 'American people think Chinese people write such sayings. They believe them.'

We laughed over them at the time, but later those fortunes were quite useful in helping me to catch a husband. An-mei introduced me to a man her husband knew, someone who attended their church and was looking for a good Chinese wife. So that is how I met Tin Jong, your father.

We were shy at first, your father and I, neither of us able to speak to each other in our different Chinese dialects. We learnt English together, and communicated in beginner's English and sign language. It's hard to tell someone's marriage intentions when you can't say things aloud. Finally An-mei suggested I give him one of the little cakes, with its paper message. I found the right one almost at once: 'A house is not a home when a wife is not at home.'

The next time I saw him, I casually offered him the cookie. As he read the writing, I asked, 'What does it say?'

'I don't know this word "wife",' he answered. 'I can look in my dictionary tonight and tell you tomorrow.'

And the next day he asked me in English, 'Lindo, can you wife me?' We laughed together over his mistake, but that is how we decided to get married.

And nine months later we had our proof of citizenship, a baby boy, your brother Winston. And two years later, Vincent. And then you. I wanted you to have the best circumstances, the best character. That's why I named you Waverly, after the street we lived in. I wanted you to think, this is where I belong.

Mr Rory has finished my hair. 'You look great, Ma,' says my daughter. 'Everyone at the wedding will think you're my sister.'

I look at my face in the mirror. I look at her face and it's the first time I have seen it. 'Ai-ya! What's happened to your nose?'

'What do you mean? It's just the same nose.'

'But why is it crooked?'

'It's your nose. You gave me this nose.'

'How can it be? You must have an operation to correct it.'

But my daughter puts her smiling face next to my worried one. 'Don't be silly. Our nose isn't so bad. It makes us look clever. It means we're looking one way, while following another.'

'People can see this in our face?'

She laughs. 'They just know we are two-faced.'

'This is good?'

'This is good if you get what you want.'

I think about our two faces. I think about my intentions. Which one is American? Which one is Chinese? Which one is better? If you show one, you must always sacrifice the other.

And now I think, What did I lose? What did I get back in return? I will ask my daughter what she thinks.

A Pair of Tickets

The minute our train leaves the Hong Kong border and enters Shenzhen, China, I feel different. I can feel the skin on my forehead warming, my blood rushing in a new way, my bones aching with a familiar old pain. And I think, my mother was right. I am becoming Chinese.

'Cannot be helped,' she used to say, when I was a teenager and firmly denied that I had any Chinese at all under my skin. There was no doubt in her mind; once you are born Chinese, you cannot help but feel and think Chinese. 'Some day you will see,' said my mother. 'It is in your blood, waiting to be allowed to come out.' But today I realize I've never really known what it means to be Chinese. I am thirty-six years old. My mother is dead and I am on a train, carrying with me her dreams of coming home. I am going to China.

I am traveling with my seventy-two-year-old father, Canning Woo. First we are going to Guangzhou, where we will visit his aunt, whom my father has not seen since he was ten years old. And I don't know if it's the thought of seeing his aunt or the pleasure of being back in China, but he looks like a young boy on holiday, so innocent and happy I want to take his hand. For the first time I can ever remember, he has tears in his eyes, as we watch the fields flash by from the train window. And I can't help myself. I also have misty eyes, as if I had seen this a long, long time ago, and had almost forgotten.

After seeing my father's aunt in Guangzhou, we will catch a

plane to Shanghai, where I will meet my two half-sisters for the first time. They are my mother's twin daughters from her first marriage, little babies she was forced to abandon on a road as she was escaping from Kweilin and the invading army in 1944.

It was only this year that someone found them and gave them my mother's address. They wrote immediately to my mother, but of course they could not know that she had died three months before, suddenly, when a blood vessel in her brain burst. So my father had been the first to open the letter, and discovered that they thought of her every day, and loved and respected her as their mother. The letter had broken his heart – these daughters calling my mother from a life he never knew – so he gave it to my mother's old friend, Auntie Lindo, and asked her to write back and tell my sisters, as gently as possible, that my mother was dead.

But instead Auntie Lindo took the letter to the Joy Luck Club, and discussed with the other aunties what should be done, because they had all known for many years about my mother's search for her twin daughters. The aunties cried over this double sadness, of losing my mother, and of discovering her daughters too late. They hoped to find some way of making my mother's dream come true. So this is what they wrote back to my sisters:

Dearest daughters, I too have never forgotten you in my memory or my heart. I never gave up hope of seeing you again. I am only sorry it has been too long. I can tell you everything about my life since I last saw you, when our family comes to see you in China . . . They signed it with my mother's name.

It wasn't until all this had been done that they first told me about my sisters, and showed me the two letters.

'They'll think she's coming, then,' I murmured.

'How can you say she is not coming in a letter?' said Auntie Lindo. 'You must be the one to tell them.'

'But when they see it's just me, they'll be so disappointed!' I said. 'Maybe they'll hate me!'

'Hate you? Cannot be. You are their sister, part of family.'

'They'll think I am responsible for her death,' I whispered, 'that she died because I didn't appreciate her.'

And Auntie Lindo looked satisfied and sad at the same time, as if this were true and I had finally realized it. She sat down and, with tears in her eyes, wrote my sisters a two-page letter.

We have arrived in Guangzhou, and now my father and I have got off the train and are in a large waiting area filled with thousands of people and suitcases. Suddenly an old woman shouts from behind me. My father turns and looks eagerly down into her face. And then his eyes widen, his face opens up and he smiles like a pleased little boy.

'*Aiyi! Aiyi!* Auntie! Auntie!' he says softly. They hold each other's hands for a long time, saying to each other, 'Look at you! You're so old! Look how old you've become!' They are crying and laughing openly, and I bite my lip, trying not to cry. I'm afraid to feel their joy, because I'm thinking how different our arrival in Shanghai will be tomorrow, how awkward it will feel.

I take a photo of my father and his aunt with the Polaroid camera I have brought. Aiyi is only five years older than my father, but she looks ancient, shrunken, skin and bones. Her thin hair is pure white, her teeth are brown and rotten. So much for stories of Chinese women looking young for ever, I tell myself.

We meet the other members of Aiyi's family. The introductions go by so fast, I can hardly remember who they all are. They have come to the station to meet us, because their village is a long way from Guangzhou, and we only have a day and a night to spend with them. They plan to stay at the hotel with us, so that we can all make the most of our time together.

Now it is one o'clock in the morning, and it seems we have been talking all day and all night, in a mixture of dialects. Some of my relations are asleep on the beds or the floor of the hotel room. Aiyi is awake, although looking sleepy, and listening to my father.

'Suyuan didn't tell me she was trying all these years to find her daughters,' he is saying. 'Naturally I did not discuss them with her. I thought she was ashamed of leaving them behind.'

'How could she give up those babies!' sighs Aiyi. 'Twin girls! We have never had such luck in our family.' And I listen carefully as she adds, 'What were they called?'

'They have their father's family name, Wang,' says my father. 'Their given names are Chwun Yu and Chwun Hwa.'

'What do their names mean?' I ask.

'One means Spring Rain, the other Spring Flower. Rain come before flower, same order these girls were born.'

'And what does Ma's name mean?' I whisper.

'The way she write Suyuan means Long-Desired Wish. But there is another way to write Suyuan. The meaning is opposite – Long-Held Grudge. When your mother get angry with me, I tell her her name should be Grudge.' My father is looking at me, tears in his eyes. 'See, I pretty clever, hah?'

I nod, wishing I could find some way to comfort him.

'Your name also special,' he says. 'Jing means excellent, best quality, purest. And Mei, well, *meimei* is younger sister.'

I think about this, my mother's long-desired wish, and me, the younger sister who was supposed to be the purest element of the others.

'So why did she abandon those babies on the road?' I ask my father. I need to know, because I feel lost too.

'No shame in what she done,' he replies. 'None.' And he goes on to tell me what really happened when my mother escaped from Kweilin. He has pieced together the information from my half-sisters' letter and his conversations with the aunties.

My mother had sewn enough money and jewellery into her silk dress to pay for rides along the road to Chungking, where her husband was at the time. But all the drivers rushed madly past, afraid to stop. She continued walking as long as she could, singing songs to her little girls, and dropping her possessions, one by one, as she became too weak to carry them.

But after several days of walking, when her hands were bleeding from carrying her babies, and she had no more food or water, she knew she could not manage another step, and did not have the strength to carry the babies any further. So she put some money and jewellery inside the babies' clothes. She took out of her pocket the photo of herself and her husband on their wedding day, and wrote on the back the babies' names and this message: *Please take care of these babies with the money and valuables provided. When it is safe to come, if you bring them to Shanghai, 9 Weichang Lu, the Li family will give you a generous reward. Li Suyuan and Wang Fuchi.* And then she touched each baby's face, and told her not to cry. She would go down the road to find some food and would be back. And without looking back, she walked down the road, half fainting and crying, thinking only of this one last hope, that her daughters would be found by a kindhearted person who would look after them. She would not allow herself to imagine anything else.

She did not remember how far she walked, when she fell, or how she was found. She was picked up off the road by American nurses, and taken to hospital in Chungking. There she discovered that her husband had died two weeks before. To come so far, to lose so much, and to find nothing! She was in the depths of despair, to think that she had been saved, and it was now too late to go back and save her babies.

It was an old countrywoman, Mei Ching, who found them, took them back to her home and looked after them. She and her husband could see the babies came from a good family, but as neither could read or write, they could not read the writing on the back of the photo.

Mei Ching loved the girls like her own daughters, but when her husband died in 1952, and the twins were eight years old, she decided it was time to find their true family. She went to Shanghai to look for 9 Weichang Lu, but she found a factory occupying the place where my mother's family home had been.

My father first met my mother at the hospital in Chungking. They married soon afterwards, and stayed in China until 1947, visiting many different cities in their search for the lost babies. Then they went to Hong Kong, and when they finally left in 1949 for the United States, my father thought my mother was even looking for her little girls on the boat.

When letters could be openly exchanged between China and the United States, she wrote at once to old friends in Shanghai and Kweilin. But by then all the street names had changed, people had died and others had moved away. Every year she wrote to different people.

'And last year,' said my father, 'I think she got a big idea in her head, to go to China and find them herself. I didn't know she was still thinking about her daughters! When she said we should go to China, I thought she just wanted to be a tourist! So I said we were too old for that, it was too late. That must have put a terrible thought in her head, that her daughters might be dead. And I think this grew bigger and bigger in her head, until it finally killed her.'

My sisters and I stand, arms round each other, laughing and crying.

We have arrived in Shanghai. I am thinking, if only my mother had lived long enough to be the one walking towards my sisters. I am so nervous I cannot even feel my face.

Somebody shouts, 'She's here!' and then I see her, with her short hair, her small body, and the back of her hand pressed hard against her mouth. And I know it's not my mother, but I remember that look. And now I see her again, two of her, crying and waving. We run toward each other, all hesitations and expectations forgotten.

'Mama, Mama,' we all murmur, as if she were among us.

My sisters look at me proudly. 'Little Sister has grown up,' says one proudly to the other. I look at their faces again and see no sign of my mother in them. But they still look familiar. And now I also see what part of me is Chinese. It is so obvious. It is my family. It is in our blood. After all these years, it can finally be allowed to come out.

My sisters and I stand, arms round each other, laughing and wiping the tears from each other's eyes. The flash of the Polaroid goes off, and my father hands me the photo. My sisters and I watch quietly together, eager to see what develops.

The grey-green surface changes to the bright colors of our three figures, sharpening and deepening all at once. And although we don't speak, I know we all see it: together we look like our mother. Her same eyes, her same mouth, open in surprise to see, at last, her long-desired wish.

GLOSSARY

amah   (in the East) a woman whose job is taking care of children

ancestor   a person in your family who lived a long time ago

belch *(n)*   a noise made by gas from the stomach coming out of the mouth (in some cultures this can show appreciation for food)

Bible   the holy book of the Christian religion

blood vessel   a tube through which blood flows in the body

calendar   a system for deciding how time is divided up into years

carat   a unit for measuring the purity of gold (the purest gold is 24 carats)

champion   the winner of a match or series of matches

check *(American)*   a printed form used to make payments from a bank account; a **checkbook** is a book of printed checks

chess   a game for two people played on a board with 32 chessmen

chopsticks   a pair of thin sticks used for eating food, especially in Asian countries

concubine   (in some societies in the past) a woman who lives with a man, in addition to his wife or wives

contract   a formal or legal agreement between two people

courtyard   a paved garden enclosed by walls

crab   a sea animal with a hard shell and eight legs, which moves sideways on land

crooked   not straight

dialect   the form of a language spoken in a particular region

dragonfly   an insect with a long thin body and two pairs of wings, often seen over water

duck   a common bird which lives on or near water

element (in this story) earth, air, fire, water, or wood (some Chinese people believe that each person is made of these things)

face, lose face to lose people's respect because of something you have done; **(have) no face** to be unworthy of people's respect

faith a strong belief in God

fate the power that is believed to control everything that happens and that cannot be stopped or changed

grudge *(n)* a feeling of anger or dislike towards someone who has treated you badly

half-sisters sisters who have one parent the same, but not both

honour *(v)* to respect; to **dishonour** is to cause the disgrace of someone, or to treat someone with disrespect

jade a hard green stone used in making jewellery and ornaments

look down on to think that you are better than another person

magpie a black and white bird with a long tail and a noisy cry

mah jong a Chinese game for four people, played with small pieces of wood with symbols on them

malignant (in this story) of something that brings evil with it

matchmaker (in this story) a person who is paid by families to find suitable husbands or wives for their children

minutes the written record of what was said at a meeting

monkey business dishonest or silly behaviour; in this story, a sexual relationship outside marriage

movie *(American)* a cinema film

net threads of rope tied loosely together, used for catching fish

noble *(adj)* belonging to a high social rank by birth

omen an event regarded as a sign of future happiness or disaster

opium a drug made from poppies, used in the past to reduce pain or help people sleep

peach-blossom the flowers of a peach tree; connected in this story with the idea of good luck

Polaroid a photo printed by the camera itself after a few seconds

prodigy a young child who has very great ability in something

rabbit a small animal with soft fur, long ears, and a short tail

rickshaw a light two-wheeled vehicle, pulled by someone walking or cycling, used to carry passengers in some Asian countries

roasted cooked in an oven, using dry heat

scar a mark left on the skin after an injury has healed

scarf a piece of cloth worn around the neck, head or shoulders

shares units of equal value into which a company is divided; people who own shares receive part of the company's profits

show off to behave in a boastful way, trying to impress people

smart clever, intelligent, quick-thinking

stage a raised area in a hall on which musicians perform

style a particular way of doing something; an understanding of high-quality appearance or design; *(adj)* **stylish**

swan a large, rather beautiful bird that is usually white, has a long thin neck, and lives on or near water

talent a natural ability to be good at something; *(adj)* **talented**

talent show a competition in which people sing, play music, etc.

turtle a large sea animal with a hard round shell

twins two children born at the same time to the same mother

water melon a large fruit with dark green skin, red flesh and black seeds

wheelbarrow an open container with a wheel and two handles, used outdoors to carry things

yin and yang the two basic principles of the universe in Chinese philosophy; **yin** is the dark, not active, female principle; **yang** is the bright active male principle

ACTIVITIES

Before Reading

1 Read the introduction on the first page of the book, and the back cover. Which of these cultural differences might cause problems for the daughters in this story, do you think? Put the problems in order of difficulty, and explain the reasons for your order.

- speaking Chinese at home and English at school
- choosing Chinese or American friends, or boyfriends
- eating Chinese food at home and American food with friends
- bringing American friends home and visiting their houses
- learning facts from their teachers and old Chinese stories from their mothers
- finding clothes which their mothers *and* friends approve of
- deciding whether to 'think Chinese' or 'think American'

2 What do you think the title *The Joy Luck Club* might refer to? Choose one or more of these answers, or think of your own.

1 A club started by a woman called Joy Luck.
2 A place where games of chance are played for money.
3 A group of people who meet to try to win luck or happiness.

3 Read the story introduction again, and discuss possible answers to these questions.

1 What kind of lives do you think the mothers had in China? What might the 'unspeakable sorrows' be that they left behind?
2 In the USA, what kind of life-styles do you think the daughters have? How are their lives different from their parents' lives?

ACTIVITIES

While Reading

Read the first chapter, *The Joy Luck Club*. Choose the best question-word for these questions, and then answer them.

Who / What / Why

1 ... was Jing-mei now the fourth player at the mah jong table?
2 ... started the Joy Luck Club in San Francisco?
3 ... did Jing-mei know her mother's Kweilin story so well?
4 ... did the women in Kweilin start playing mah jong?
5 ... did Suyuan use to push her babies and her belongings in?
6 ... did Suyuan have when she arrived in Chungking?
7 ... had Suyuan been searching for, for so many years?
8 ... provided the money for Jing-mei's trip to China?
9 ... does Jing-mei promise her aunties?

Read *The Joy Luck Club* again, *Scar*, *The Red Candle*, and *The Moon Lady*. Then answer these questions.

1 Which mothers were young children, and which were young women, when they experienced the events in their stories?
2 Which of the mothers' experiences do *you* think was the hardest to live through and to deal with? Why do you think that?

Before you read on, can you guess the answer to these questions?

1 Will Jing-mei go to China, or will her sisters come to America?
2 Will she write to tell her sisters that their mother is dead, or only tell them the news when she meets them?
3 Will the meeting be joyful, or awkward and full of bitterness?

Read *Rules of the Game, The Voice from the Wall, Without Wood* and *Best Quality*. Who said this to whom? What were they talking about, or what do you think they really meant by these words?

Rules of the Game
1 'Wise man, he not go against wind. Strongest wind cannot be seen.'
2 'It's just so embarrassing.'
3 'He gave me this from his heart.'
4 'You blow from the north, south, east and west. Then other person becomes confused.'

The Voice from the Wall
1 'When something goes against your nature, you are not in balance.'
2 'We do this kind of thing all the time.'
3 'It's something we started before we got married.'
4 'Then why don't you stop it?'

Without Wood
1 'Forgive us for his bad manners.'
2 'You must try. This is your fate, what you must do.'
3 'If someone tells you what to do, then you are not trying.'
4 'You can't just pull me out of your life and throw me away.'

Best Quality
1 'Of course you can be prodigy, too.'
2 'You lucky you don't have this problem.'
3 'Maybe I could afford his prices, if your company paid me on time.'
4 'This is your life's importance.'

Before you read more stories of the mothers' lives, can you guess what happens? Read the questions below, and suggest the answers you prefer, or that you think are the most likely.

1 When An-mei's grandmother Popo died, what happened to An-mei? Did she stay with her auntie, or go to live in Wu Tsing's house, where her mother was a number three concubine?

2 Before Ying-ying married St Clair and went to America, she had a Chinese husband. Did this husband die in an accident? Did he treat Ying-ying badly? Did Ying-ying have a child by him?

3 When Lindo escaped from her marriage to Tyan-yu, she sailed for America. Did she choose her next husband herself? Why did they have a baby as quickly as possible?

Read *Magpies, Waiting Between the Trees, Double Face* and *A Pair of Tickets*. Are these sentences true (T) or false (F)? Rewrite the false sentences with more accurate information.

1 The turtle's message to An-mei was that crying is helpful, and makes you feel better.

2 An-mei's mother was proud to be Wu Tsing's concubine.

3 An-mei's mother planned her own death.

4 Ying-ying remembered her first husband with fondness and regret, and wished that his unborn baby had lived.

5 Ying-ying thought that her daughter had poor eyesight.

6 Lindo wanted her children to have Chinese circumstances and an American character.

7 When Lindo first met her second husband, neither of them could speak the other's language.

8 Suyuan had given her twin babies to an old countrywoman.

9 Jing-mei and her sisters all look like their mother.

ACTIVITIES

After Reading

1 These groups of sentences are about the lives of the mothers in the story. Which mother is being described each time? Join the sentences together to make paragraphs, using linking words like these and making any other appropriate changes.

and / and so / and then / and when / but / so that /
soon afterwards / that / when / where / who

1 She was married. She had twin daughters. The Japanese army invaded China. She escaped from a town called Kweilin. She left her daughters on the road. She was taken to hospital. She heard her husband was dead. She met and married another man.

2 Her father died. Her mother became the concubine of a rich man. The child was nine years old. She went to live with her mother at the rich man's house. Later, her mother poisoned herself, choosing the day carefully. The rich man would have to bring up the child as his own. She grew up. She married. She went to live in the USA. She had seven children.

3 Her parents arranged a marriage for her. She was twelve years old. She was sent to live with her future in-laws. It was not a happy life. After a few years she managed to persuade her mother-in-law. The marriage contract should be broken. She moved to the USA. She married again.

4 She married a man. He deceived her. He abandoned her. This made her so unhappy. She killed her unborn baby. Many years later she met an American. She married him. They went to the USA. She never really recovered from losing her first child.

2 **Which daughter is connected to each of these events or objects (there are three for each daughter)? Then say what effect the events have on the daughters' lives, and what importance the objects hold for them.**

- asking for salted fruit
- a check for $10,000
- a chess set
- an overgrown garden
- a bed next to a wall
- having piano lessons
- death of a brother, by drowning
- eating too much ice cream
- a crab with a missing leg
- a badly-made table
- a fur jacket
- a piece of jade on a gold chain

3 **Here are some thoughts of people in the story. Who is thinking? Complete the thoughts with one suitable word for each gap.**

1 'She looks so _____! Well, she had to know sometime. It's her _____, too, in a way. They're her sisters. And when I find them – because I know I will, it's just a question of _____, – we'll all be together, a _____ of five!'

2 'How could he refuse a second _____? He ate nothing! What a _____ young man! A bad husband for my daughter. But what can I do? I _____ her how to live with Americans. Now she wants to _____ one!'

3 'What is this? Why do they write down what each one has _____? Why does it _____ who buys the ice cream? Everything is out of _____ in this house. It will _____ into pieces, like their _____. And my daughter _____ see any of the signs.'

4 'Hnnh! Now I understand. My daughter's husband feels guilty about something. That's why he's sent her a _____. And what do husbands feel guilty about? Other _____, of course! She won't _____ me when I tell her, but a mother always _____.'

4 **When Jing-mei meets her sisters, Chwun Yu and Chwun Hwa, what does she tell them about her childhood and the mother they never knew? Complete Jing-mei's side of their conversation.**

CHWUN YU: So, little sister! We only learnt we had a sister when your Auntie Lindo wrote to us. But you must have known about us all your life.

JING-MEI: _____

CHWUN HWA: Her Kweilin story? What was that?

JING-MEI: _____

CHWUN YU: And so the new ending was all about us, was it?

JING-MEI: _____

CHWUN HWA: Aii-ya! A wheelbarrow! Those were terrible days. Did Mama tell you many stories about her life in China?

JING-MEI: _____

CHWUN YU: The same story? That shows how much Mama was thinking about us!

JING-MEI: _____

CHWUN HWA: Yes, your Auntie Lindo told us that in her letter. But all the street names were changed, you see, little sister. That's why it was so difficult to find us.

JING-MEI: _____

CHWUN YU: Yes, we dreamed of finding her again too. So sad for her. But she had you – you were a great comfort to her.

JING-MEI: _____

CHWUN HWA: Disappointment? I'm sure that's not true!

JING-MEI: _____

CHWUN YU: It's very hard to be a really good pianist, you know.

JING-MEI: _____

CHWUN HWA: But you mustn't feel guilty. She was a good mother to you, and I'm sure she loved you just as you were.

5　There are four texts in this book which are not part of the story, but which illustrate some of the ideas in it. Read the texts, and then match them with the statements below. Are the statements accurate summaries of the texts, do you think? If not, how would you change them? Do you agree with the ideas? Why, or why not?

> *Feathers from a Thousand Miles Away* (page 1)
> *The Twenty-Six Malignant Gates* (page 34)
> *American Translation* (page 35)
> *Queen Mother of the Western Skies* (page 78)

1　Children should always listen to their mother's warnings.
2　Mothers always want their children to have a better life than they had.
3　Mothers often look back and worry that they have not brought up their children in the best way.
4　Mothers can never stop giving advice to their adult children.

6　**Did you like this story? Discuss your answers to these questions.**

1　In your opinion, which mother and daughter had the best relationship, and which the worst? Explain why you think this.
2　Which woman did you most admire or feel sorry for, and why? If they were real people, which would you most like to meet?
3　Did you find these moments in the story moving, satisfying, dramatic, unexpected? Describe your reactions to each one.
  • Jing-mei receiving the aunties' check
  • Waverly telling her mother she is going to marry Rich
  • Lena's loneliness after her mother lost her baby
  • Rose telling Ted that she was going to keep the house
  • An-mei's loss of faith when she realizes Bing is dead
  • Jing-mei meeting her sisters in China

ABOUT THE AUTHOR

Amy Tan was born in Oakland, California, in 1952, a few years after her parents emigrated to the USA from China. In 1972 she graduated with an English and Linguistics degree, and went on to do an MA in Linguistics. First she worked as a language consultant for projects involving disabled children. Then she became a freelance business writer for several large companies.

She started writing fiction when she joined a writers' workshop, and her first short story, *End Game*, appeared in 1986. She continued to write, and visited China for the first time in 1987, experiencing exactly what her mother had described: 'As soon as my feet touched China, I became Chinese.' *The Joy Luck Club*, originally written as a collection of linked stories, was published in 1989. Through word-of-mouth recommendations, it became a surprise bestseller. It received a number of awards and was adapted into a feature film in 1994.

Amy Tan's second book, *The Kitchen God's Wife*, came out in 1991, followed by *The Hundred Secret Senses* in 1995. A fourth novel, *The Bonesetter's Daughter*, was published in 2001. Her short stories and essays have appeared in magazines, and she has also written two children's books. Her familiarity with both Chinese and American cultural backgrounds has given her an insight into the way people communicate, and there is humour as well as sadness in the way she describes those moments where the two very different cultures meet.

Like the novelist Stephen King and others, she is a member of the literary garage band, *The Rock Bottom Remainders*. With them she sings the Nancy Sinatra classic, *These Boots Are Made for Walking*, to raise money for charity. She lives in San Francisco and New York with her husband.

OXFORD BOOKWORMS LIBRARY

Classics • Crime & Mystery • Factfiles • Fantasy & Horror
Human Interest • Playscripts • Thriller & Adventure
True Stories • World Stories

The OXFORD BOOKWORMS LIBRARY provides enjoyable reading in English, with a wide range of classic and modern fiction, non-fiction, and plays. It includes original and adapted texts in seven carefully graded language stages, which take learners from beginner to advanced level. An overview is given on the next pages.

All Stage 1 titles are available as audio recordings, as well as over eighty other titles from Starter to Stage 6. All Starters and many titles at Stages 1 to 4 are specially recommended for younger learners. Every Bookworm is illustrated, and Starters and Factfiles have full-colour illustrations.

The OXFORD BOOKWORMS LIBRARY also offers extensive support. Each book contains an introduction to the story, notes about the author, a glossary, and activities. Additional resources include tests and worksheets, and answers for these and for the activities in the books. There is advice on running a class library, using audio recordings, and the many ways of using Oxford Bookworms in reading programmes. Resource materials are available on the website <www.oup.com/elt/bookworms>.

The *Oxford Bookworms Collection* is a series for advanced learners. It consists of volumes of short stories by well-known authors, both classic and modern. Texts are not abridged or adapted in any way, but carefully selected to be accessible to the advanced student.

You can find details and a full list of titles in the *Oxford Bookworms Library Catalogue* and *Oxford English Language Teaching Catalogues*, and on the website <www.oup.com/elt/bookworms>.